6 99
599

Drover
and the
Zebras

Books by Bill Granger

NOVELS

Drover and the Zebras
Drover
The November Man
Schism
The Shattered Eye
The British Cross
The Zurich Numbers
Hemingway's Notebook
There Are No Spies
The Infant of Prague
The Man Who Heard Too Much
League of Terror
The Last Good German
Time for Frankie Coolin
Public Murders
Newspaper Murders
Priestly Murders
The El Murders
Sweeps
Queen's Crossing

NONFICTION

The Magic Feather*
Fighting Jane*
Lords of the Last Machine*
Chicago Pieces

(*with Lori Granger)

DROVER AND THE ZEBRAS

The New Drover Novel

Bill Granger

William Morrow and Company, Inc.   New York

It is the policy of William Morrow and Company, Inc., and its imprints and affiliates,
recognizing the importance of preserving what has been written, to print the books
we publish on acid-free paper, and we exert our best efforts to that end.

Library of Congress Cataloging-in-Publication Data

Granger, Bill.
    Drover and the zebras / by Bill Granger.
        p.   cm.
    ISBN 0-688-09857-6
    I. Title.
PS3557.R256D77   1992
813'.54–dc20   91-43827
                                                CIP

Printed in the United States of America

First Edition

1 2 3 4 5 6 7 8 9 10

BOOK DESIGN BY LYNN DONOFRIO DESIGNS

This is for two great
sportswriters—
Jerome Holtzman
and
Ray Sons—
who encouraged the kid
along the way

CHARACTERS IN
DROVER AND THE ZEBRAS

Fionna Givens—who lures Drover into helping her brother avoid a basketball recruiting scandal

Paul Givens—head coach at St. Mary's who tries to be a Boy Scout in a sport gone out of control

Father O'Brien—who runs St. Mary's but prefers to keep his head in the sand when it comes to sports in school

Steve March—a Mob collector who loses control from time to time

Leo Myers—the scared bookie at the center of a point-shaving scandal

Dan Briggs—a college zebra (referee) who kills himself after getting questions from the NCAA

Neil O'Neill—who coached St. Mary's before Paul and has gone on to a television life of money and women and games

Black Kelly—the retired fireman and Drover's landlord who wants to visit Chicago for an old home week

Drover—the ex-sportswriter-turned-knight-errant for a lady with real distress

Captain Carmody—a retired cop who put Drover through college and who used to murder hoodlums on the side

Peterson—the FBI guy who warns off Drover and the NCAA from a little game of his own making

"Remember, pal, this is no dress rehearsal."
—The Gapper behind the Green Door

ONE

THEY WERE in Chicago this December and there was snow in the gutters. Old home week for both of them, over twenty-two hundred miles east of their usual place of exile on the pier in Santa Cruz. There was always snow in their memories of where they had both come from, even when the California sun usually baked them on Christmas Day. Snow was home.

Drover was crammed on the bench halfway up the west balcony of the old gym on Belden and Black Kelly was doing part of the cramming. Kelly held the outside seat, his foot in the aisle, because he said his foot needed to "breathe." His bulk had shoved down the row of cheering collegians and Drover was between a rock and rockers.

DePaul was in the process of running up the score against Creighton. Frank Bonhoffer, the DePaul University coach, was screaming from the sidelines to slow it down but he might as well have been an oak falling in a deserted forest. Basketball is like that—sometimes you throw the plans away and just do it.

The rest of the four thousand in the seats—along with his team—were ignoring him. This is called alley basketball in some cities and street ball in others: It's when the game gets down to pure instinct, undirected, five athletes moving like five fingers in a piano exercise, striking all the right keys without reading the notes.

Kelly was grunting, as close as he ever came to a scream. Drover was studying it, elbows on knees and chin in hands, watching the cool of Marcus Garvey as he maneuvered inside the key and suddenly twisted and leapt in one motion, arcing the ball in a lazy half circle into the basket. Two more unneeded points; DePaul was up by eighteen.

The crowd screamed for eighty. Two burly male cheerleaders, surrounded by companion drumbeaters of the opposite sex, bellowed the simple chant: "De-Paul! De-Paul!"

"You aren't very excited," Kelly said.

"I'm excited," Drover said in a flat voice. The old gym roared around him and the noise pounded off the vaulted ceiling and pushed back down on the tops of their heads. The sound was like fireworks and you could have sworn you saw colors in the roar.

"Are we watching the same game?"

"What game? Garvey is practicing for his NBA tryout. Bonhoffer won't be able to keep the kid for his senior year."

Black Kelly squinted, making his baby blues that much bluer. "You analyze too much. You think he should graduate and become the rocket scientist he was aiming to be?"

"I'll bet the school hates the gate. I know Creighton will. Not to mention the NCAA. Four thousand for a class A school won't pay airfare to the Final Four."

"That's commerce, Drover. Get in the swing of it. This is sport."

"Yeah. Sport."

The gym had been built in 1955 when basketball was a game in college and the Final Four, like the Super Bowl, was not even in the cards. DePaul usually played home games in Rosemont Horizon which was not even in Chicago. But the Horizon had been closed for two weeks for emergency repairs and the Chicago Stadium was otherwise occupied with the Chicago Bulls and the DePaul Blue Demons had returned to their ancient roots for an evening in the old neighborhood of the city by the El tracks. It was as falsely quaint as a stroll through Main Street in Disneyland.

Garvey again. He stole the pass at midcourt, sending up another round of fireworks. It was all his and he made it show, pounding down the court with pro steps and punching the ball through the hoop with a hammer.

Twenty up.

Time.

The Creighton irregulars straggled to the far sideline to get towels and bomb damage assessment. Bad enough to lose; worse to get a small house with attendant small change for playing Christians to the lions.

"I'm going to take a walk," Drover said, standing up.

Kelly swung both legs into the aisle. "You got no school spirit."

"I didn't go to DePaul."

"I didn't graduate but what difference does it make? We're from Chicago."

"See you later at Maguire's."

Kelly said nothing. Drover took the steps to the exit tunnel and then down more steps to the bare concourse. The gym was called Alumni Hall and in the quiet of practice afternoons, you could hear the Els go by one hundred feet to the east. He had looked forward to the games—they had caught the Blackhawks in hockey two days before and the Bulls the night before—and for a chance to see the old hometown from the street level of an old neighborhood. Now he just felt indifferent. The outsider in him was coming out again, Kelly might say.

He went through the Kenmore Street exit door and stood for a moment inhaling the cool December air. There were piles of dirty snow in the gutters. The breeze smelled of more snow coming. He hunched into his windbreaker and turned east. Maguire's was a campus saloon, if you could say that a university parked in the middle of a city neighborhood had a campus and if you could ignore the elevated tracks that ran through it and right over the saloon.

Maybe he was feeling down because every time he came back to Chicago, everything had changed, grown older, sometimes grown better and sometimes grown worse. He had left the city a long time ago and like Sinatra says, it kept tuggin' his sleeve.

13

"Jimmy. Jimmy."

The voice was out of breath. He turned and saw the woman shaded by the orange streetlights. The El rumbled against the skyline, above the tennis courts. They were the only people left on Sheffield Avenue for the moment.

"Jimmy, don't you remember me?"

He smiled and saw things all changed again, the way everything was changed. Reunions and old home weeks are designed that way, to lacerate. Like this woman with her pretty, pretty face and unforgettable eyes and slight streak of gray in her raven hair. Angels don't get gray, not ever.

"Fionna," she said, standing near him, her words punched out with puffs of breath. "Fionna Givens."

"I know," Drover said.

She kissed him on the cheek, just like old home weekers do. She gave him the same kind of hug. He had to smile. Fionna Givens felt very nice to hug. Always had. Maybe there was something to nostalgia after all.

"You're going to Maguire's," she said.

"To see if it's still standing."

"The last real thing in this neighborhood except for St. Vincent's church. The yuppies own everything else. We're gentrified."

"I noticed walking around. Even the gangways look safe."

She gave him a smile. Hers was sharp, everything about her face was sharp and even a little cunning. Cats look that way, even when they're cuddly kittens. Drover and Fionna Givens were beyond the kitten stage and they knew it, but facial habits die hard.

"I was wondering how I'd get to see you. I called your hotel. I guessed you might come to the game because you were with Kelly. Black Kelly. I—"

Something stopped her. It was the look on Drover's face. Drover didn't intend it to show.

Instead, she took his arm and bundled against it. "There's a coffeehouse on Webster. Do you think you could buy me a cup of coffee?"

"You on the wagon?"

14

Eyes narrowed and looked at the sidewalk. "I need a quiet place. I need a little time to talk to you, Jimmy."

"Never turn down a lady," Drover said. He thought he kept it light. He felt her bundling body next to his arm and hip. It made walking a little awkward but Drover didn't mind as long as she didn't. Old home week. Always full of surprises.

"What do you want to talk about?"

She stopped and he had to stop. Fionna suddenly kissed him, right on the lips. Her lips were very moist and this was not a kiss from your sister.

Drover felt scared then.

Fionna was a married woman.

And all the trouble in the world was in her eyes.

TWO

THE GIRL with purple hair had coked-out eyes. She brought them two *cafés américains* which translated to coffee regular at two bucks a cup. She forced her eyes to blink when she put the bill on the table between them. Drover waited for her to go away and then decided she wanted money up front. It's hard to communicate with the walking dead, when even the simplest transactions require you to do all the work. Ask someone who sells hot dogs at a Grateful Dead concert.

When Coke Eyes walked away in her black tights and loose overshirt, Drover was slow in looking at Fionna. He stared at his coffee instead. Priests do this in confessionals: They don't look at the penitent, they stare off into darkness and listen to the voice.

"I couldn't find you in that crowd at first and then I saw you stand up. I thought I'd miss you. A perfect ending to a rotten day," she said.

"You found me." Nothing in the voice except tone. He looked

at her. Her eyes were green but they had lost some color. Maybe it was the night or the coming winter.

"I remember the first time I saw you, well, the first time I remembered seeing you, you were doing the same thing. St. Mary's was winning big and you got up in the middle of the game which nobody ever did who went to St. Mary's and you walked out. I thought you were odd. I mean, who didn't like to see his team roll up a score."

"Me," said Drover. He stirred the coffee and took out the spoon. It tasted pretty good, almost with a French touch to it.

"Still the same."

"Nothing's the same," Drover said. *"Salut'."*

He toasted her with the porcelain cup and swallowed some.

"You're right. Nothing's the same." Tasted her coffee and made a bitter face. The place had palm plants and Janis Joplin on the background track. It might have been 1966.

"How's Neil?"

Cautiously, prying the edges.

"Nothing's the same," Fionna Givens said. She put down her cup. She looked at him and took a cigarette pack out of her purse. She selected one and lit it with a plastic Light Stick.

He waited while she exhaled.

"Neil and I are separated," Fionna said.

"Oh."

Silence. Janis was making sex to the mike insofar as sex was made in the olden days, pre-MTV.

"Irish divorce," Fionna said. "Well, it was. Now it's going to lawyers."

"Oh," Drover said. It was the only line he could think of.

"Neil is working for ESPN this year."

"I heard."

"You hear everything where you work, don't you?" Like an accusation.

"Where I work? I don't work, Fionna. My sportswriting days are over."

"I heard."

"You hear everything where you work too?"

"Jesus, Jimmy." Soft, a plea against hurt. Don't hit me again. "Everything turns out a mess."

He looked at his coffee cup again because he didn't want to see her pain. He picked up the spoon and stirred and took the spoon out of the cup and laid it down on the table. When he looked at Fionna again, she was watching him. He cleared his throat.

"How's your brother, Paul?"

Her turn to look down. But she spoke up while she did it.

"I wanted to see you about Paul."

The priest in the confessional stared right at the penitent through the screen. He saw the sinner and wasn't hearing the sins right now. She had pain in her eyes and that's what had taken away some of the color.

"I had to . . . approach you. Paul wouldn't."

"Paul was never my friend."

"I think Paul liked you."

"I didn't care. He resented that I went out with you."

"He never said it."

"What was he going to say? Don't go out with Drover?"

"No. Paul wouldn't have said that. He was my older brother but he wasn't bossy at all."

Drover let it drop. Whatever Fionna had to tell him wasn't about dating in college.

"We had some good times, didn't we?" Fionna said, not letting it go.

Not that many. A few. They stood out. And then Fionna found someone else one day and he was on the basketball court and not in the stands and that was that. Neil O'Neill was as good as gold on the basketball court at St. Mary's and that was very golden indeed. It wasn't his fault that St. Mary's couldn't keep up with his speed and finesse and fine sense of shooting. Neil had known his limitations by instinct and never took a shot he didn't have a lock on. No one else at St. Mary's was as good, though, and St. Mary's ended up in the NIT for three straight years instead of the NCAA finals. He even had a year in the pros, as a bench guard for the Knicks. The game even then was getting too big for someone only six three. So he had married Fionna and done time as an assistant at Wesleyan and then taken the big job as head coach of St. Mary's. Until this year and until ESPN caught him as a color commentator.

Fionna noticed the silence and noticed the ruminations in Drover's sad brown eyes. Big brown eyes she had said once, tracing his eyebrows with her fingertips after they had made love.

"Paul needs to see you but he can't bend enough."

"Like I said, we weren't buddies."

"He's in bad trouble, Jimmy."

"Bad enough for you to track me down."

"I knew Black Kelly's sister from this neighborhood. I didn't know you knew him. She mentioned once that her brother was running a restaurant in Santa Cruz, California." She said it all out, excluding only the zip code. "Then one day she brings up your name, says a guy named Drover was living out in Santa Cruz too and that he used to be a sportswriter here in Chicago. I told her I knew you and she told me all about you. I don't think she approved that her brother knew you. She said you were sort of a shady character. I couldn't imagine such a thing."

"She told you I had dealings with a man in Vegas, that's why you brought up Vegas."

"No." Shook her head, tasted her cigarette, looked around. The sinner looked away. "Paul knew that."

Drover nodded, considering it. "Paul might. I scout his team."

"For gamblers."

"He has a very good team. People even bet on college teams. Shocking but true. A guy paid me a fee to scout St. Mary's this year, see if they had a chance at the Final Four."

"Do they?"

"You know as well as I do."

"They're going all the way."

"It just might happen."

"Oh, Jimmy. This is very bad and I don't have any right to put it on you but I'm grabbing at straws. Paul just sleepwalks through it. It's tearing him apart but he handles it inside."

"What's so bad?"

Fionna stared at him for a moment. "Neil. I thought Neil quit as coach of St. Mary's last year because of the broadcasting offer. He told everyone he was tired of coaching. He recommended Paul for the job. He was so nice to Paul, I was amazed. I mean, when we separated three years ago, it wasn't so pleasant. There had been a lot of shouting and screaming. And other things."

She paused and lit another cigarette. The puff of smoke was accompanied by a cough. She shook her head. "I quit for five years and now I'm back at it."

Drover waited and said nothing.

"He shafted Paul."

The trouble with a priest in the confessional is that he doesn't get the good lines. He has to wait for the monologue to go on.

"The NCAA got some material four weeks ago about a fix, something about point shaving with two or three of the players."

"What do you mean, material?"

"A letter. Listing names and dates and games. The letter was anonymous."

"Then it's horseshit. The NCAA gets allegations like that all the time about all kinds of people."

She shook her head. "They took it seriously. They started with a referee mentioned. Dan Briggs. They called him in and talked to him. He was pretty shaken, Paul said, and he denied being part of any kind of fix, denied knowing gamblers, all of it."

"So?"

"So he killed himself the next day."

Drover let it soak in and then shook his head. "A guy killed himself because some anonymous finger pointer set him up with the NCAA? That doesn't make any sense, Fionna."

"It doesn't make sense to the NCAA either. They were going through the motions up to the minute Dan Briggs committed suicide."

"He leave a note?"

"He left a note."

"What'd the note say?"

"It rambled a bit. It said something about doing bad things for good reasons. It asked that his family forgive him. Dan Briggs had a grown son. His wife was dead."

"How old was he?"

"Fifty-three."

"What was he? In real life?"

"Insurance broker."

"He should of known that insurance doesn't pay out in suicides."

"That isn't the point, Jimmy." She clutched his sleeve. "The point is, the NCAA investigators are all over St. Mary's in the last two weeks."

"Why don't I know this? Like you said, I should have heard something about this."

"Because no one knows about it yet. It won't stay that way much longer but St. Mary's is kind of isolated."

"Tell me," Drover said. "Six buildings in a cornfield."

"If St. Mary's gets a bad mark, the program is finished. The school couldn't ride out a suspension," Fionna said.

"And if players shaved points in games, the team would be shut down," Drover said. "And that includes your brother, Paul."

Fionna said, "All Paul ever wanted was to be head coach of St. Mary's. I'm not saying he wouldn't get another job somewhere or that the school would blame him. . . . But St. Mary's needs what they're going to get this year. They need the Final Four, they need to get invited to a conference next year. The days of the independent schools are over."

"You're very smart about sports," Drover said.

"You get that way when you have a brother like Paul," Fionna said. "I love him."

"I know."

Waited. Janis Joplin was talking about her sex life with Bobby McGee and throwing in the F word under the music. Freeze frame. Abbie Hoffman might walk in the door in the next minute.

"Why did you say Neil did it?"

"Don't you see? He hates me and he hates my brother and he sent that letter to the NCAA—"

"He say he did?"

Fionna shook her head. "I called him in New York. He laughed at me and said I must be drunk."

"Were you drunk?"

"It was one in the morning. Paul had poured out his heart to me. He can't tell Betsy."

"Who's that?"

"His wife." Fionna lit another cigarette. "She's nice. That's the best word for her. They have two children and they're just beautiful. But he can't talk to her the way he can talk to me."

"So you got drunk and called up your ex-husband."

"Still my husband. He's finally getting around to the divorce. He didn't want a divorce while he was still coaching at St. Mary's. Father O'Brien wouldn't have permitted it."

Drover said, "He's not the pope and Neil isn't Henry the Eighth, Fionna. Modern times."

"Modern times at St. Mary's? Father O would like nothing better than to close down the basketball program, except it pays half the faculty salaries. St. Mary's is a backwater."

"I knew it when we went there," Drover said.

"Why did you go then?"

"I hate to tell you."

She waited.

"A guy sent me there."

"A guy?"

"A guy."

"What guy?"

"Captain Carmody."

"Captain of what?"

"Captain of cops. He was self-appointed protector of our little family group, Ma and me. He explained it to Ma and Ma bought it and I didn't have a say in it."

"That was very generous—"

"Carmody was a widower and Ma was a widow. I think it was an Irish way of putting the hit on her. Anyway, he came up with this scholarship—"

"A lot of money—"

Drover shook his head. "Never pay for what you can steal."

"What does that mean?"

"I'll tell you when I know you better."

Another silence. Janis Joplin's voice, roughed-in with drugs and booze, sandpapered the fine lyrics until they were suitable for framing. The zombie in tights and overshirt stopped at their table and asked them if they wanted more coffee. They shook their heads and she went away.

"There's nothing I can do if kids fixed games last season. They did it, they did it and the school'll suffer. And Paul. Paul's a big boy, Fionna, how old is he?"

"That isn't the point, Jimmy. He talked to them, to the three players named in the letter and they swear they never shaved points, one of them was crying."

"And no one in the joint ever did the crime," Drover said.

"Look into it. You've got all those gambling contacts—"

"I don't have gambling contacts, Fionna. I do work for a legal bookie in Vegas from time to time. He's not my boss. I'm his . . . permanent free-lance."

"A man killed himself over this."

"I don't believe it."

She gaped at him. Then: "What do you mean? Dan Briggs is dead. D-E-A-D."

"Over what? Point shaving? I can tell you a dozen stories about coaches and careers that did nothing but take off after a lot worse things. Besides, being a zebra is a part-time gig. What would it do, hurt his legitimate business? Something else was up, not that," Drover said.

She bit her lip and thought about it. "Maybe I was just too close to this."

"Maybe."

"Won't you look into it? At least make a few phone calls?"

"For you? Anything. But if I start, Fionna, it won't stop with me. And it won't be secret. The more people you talk to, the more people will talk."

"I know it, but it isn't going to be a secret much longer. It only takes one reporter on one newspaper."

"Just so you know. Just so Paul knows."

"Paul wants to talk to you."

"All right."

"The team plays Syracuse tomorrow night, regional television out east. Then they're back at St. Mary's Thursday."

Drover nodded. "Meantime, I'll call around."

"Thank you."

Quiet. Janis stopped singing.

"Walk me home?" she said.

"Sure."

"I'll give you a drink when we get there."

"Best offer," Drover said. Suddenly, he was twenty years old and she didn't have a gray streak in her black hair and they might be talking about Wittgenstein one minute and kissing the next. Soft wet kisses. The kiss she had given him on the street.

They rose and made noise with their chairs screeching on the wooden planking. The zombie stared at them or at some private vision.

"The worst thing," she said suddenly, catching his arm, holding it close to her. They stood at the door. Snow was falling. "The worst thing is the letter they got two days ago. They told Paul about it right away."

"What are you telling me?"

"Paul."

He waited.

"The second letter said Paul was part of the fixes," Fionna Givens said.

THREE

"How're the Bulls?"

That was the thing about Fox Vernon back in Vegas. His idea of small talk was recitation of the Monday morning line in football season; he had the manners of an eccentric math professor, which is what he had wanted to be before he figured out how to become a sports book and line maker.

"Worth every cent it'll cost you to have me scout them."

There was that Fox Vernon pause on the line then, the one where Vernon sits at his end with his mouth closed and his eyes staring at a computer screen, waiting for human words to continue the thought.

"Joke," Drover said. He was sitting in his underwear on the side of the hotel room bed. "Bulls are exactly what you see, about the best there is on any given night. I went to watch DePaul beat up Creighton tonight."

"How's Marcus Garvey?" Fox Vernon said. He was all business, all the time.

"Number one or two draft next spring," Drover said. "If they make it to the Final Four with him, Coach Bonhoffer might be able to convince the kid to stay with DePaul one more year. But I doubt it."

"Which part do you doubt?" Fox Vernon said. He was a University of Chicago grad, brilliant with numbers and enticed by sports like an ordinary sports fan. His was one of nearly a hundred legal books in Las Vegas. He was an independent, which meant he might rub shoulders with the Mob in hotel lobbies but he didn't go to their weddings or bar mitzvahs. He and Drover had an arrangement: Drover watched sports with the critical eye of a sportswriter and The Foxman tapped his thoughts from time to time for a fee.

"I doubt DePaul can make it to the Four with a one-man show. Marcus is selfish because he's immature and because his team isn't up to his standards."

"Sounds like the old Chicago Bulls with the Jordan Magic Show," Fox Vernon said.

"Somewhat. But Marcus, good as he is, isn't Michael Jordan and you, of all people, should know that you can't even talk about college ball and NBA ball being remotely the same game," Drover said. "Point two is that Marcus wants to be in the Big Show bad and spending another year in Remedial Finger Painting One-oh-two can't hold a candle to that. It was a nice game otherwise. They played in the old Alumni Hall and the joint was rocking."

"You like the Bears Sunday?"

"I always like the Bears because I'm a Chicago chauvinist temporarily living in California," Drover said. "But the over is very steep. I think I'd pass on it for Sunday."

"So would I, if I were a betting man," Fox Vernon said. He wasn't joking; he never joked. He set lines, he let Drover write sports gambling books with his name on them, and he booked bets, but it was like a nondrinker running a saloon. It was safer that way.

"But that isn't why I called," Drover said. He had been thinking about it all the way back to the Drake Hotel, after he had left Fionna Givens. What would he tell Fox Vernon?

"What is it?"

"I met an old girlfriend tonight."

"And you're getting married?"

"She's still married. Sort of. Fionna Givens. Took her name back when she split from Neil O'Neill."

"He looks smart on ESPN. Doesn't bounce like Dick Vitale. I hate bouncing."

"It upsets your stomach. Imagine what it does to Vitale."

"What did Neil O'Neill's ex-wife say?"

"They're separated." Pause. This time, it was Drover doing the pausing. "You hear about a college ref named Dan Briggs who killed himself?"

"Midwest conference. Shot his own head off with a double-barrel. In his rec room." Fox Vernon sounded like Joe Friday when he was combing his memory. He remembered everything, even the stuff he wanted to forget.

"You hear anything about it?"

"Is there something I should have heard?"

"I don't know," Drover said. He squinted at the digital clock on the table. Almost midnight, just a normal wake-up hour in Vegas. Here there was snow falling and the quiet that grips big northern cities on weekday December nights. Drover suddenly felt sorry for himself, a common indulgence for middle-aged people who still live in hotel rooms and forget where home is.

"The old girlfriend," Fox Vernon prompted.

"She said she heard around that there was a letter to the board of governors about some point shaving. Maybe involving a ref."

Silence. Not a pause this time but a full-blown silence.

"Who shaved what?"

"I don't know."

"I'd like to know."

"Someone is going to whisper something to someone about this. Why does a zebra kill himself?"

"College zebras are vulnerable. Part-time guys. They move in small circles, not coast to coast. They ref because they loved the game and couldn't get enough of it. It's the show biz side of their lives," Fox Vernon said. He said it in the flat, distracted voice that meant he was searching his computer memory for something.

"See what you hear about Dan Briggs," Drover said.

"And what are you going to do?"

"See what I hear about Dan Briggs."

"We'll compare notes," Fox Vernon said.

"Sure."

"Drover?"

"Yeah."

"What is Fionna Givens in all this? Where does she get her information?"

"That seems obvious."

"If her husband or ex-husband knows about this, why doesn't the world know through his commentaries on ESPN?"

"I don't know. Maybe it isn't true. Maybe lots of things." He wasn't going to tell Fox that Fionna said the information came from her brother, Paul. Let him think what he thinks.

"Givens. Givens. Is that her brother, Paul Givens, the one who succeeded O'Neill at St. Mary's?"

"The same." Another pause that wasn't pregnant but represented an act of aborting a line of thought.

"St. Mary's is serious, isn't it?" Fox Vernon said. He said it so innocently that Drover knew he was being crooked.

"I saw them the other night. They looked serious. Balance and power. Paul Givens got them to shoot the ball around even. It's a team with a capital Rah-rah. Strong posts and a good outside shooter, little white guy named Polanski. The center, this Rahway, is a tad clumsy but he's got the height."

"Final Four."

"I'd be surprised if they weren't."

"This involves St. Mary's? This other thing? About shaving?"

Drover said nothing.

"Christ. Shaving on a team that good." Fox Vernon said it sadly, as if it were a fact.

"I'm not sure of anything. I want to be sure." He let his voice drop a tone. "You want to be sure. Don't give scandal, that's what Father O'Brien taught in theology."

"You listened, didn't you? I never took a theology course."

"It shows. I try to do the right thing," Drover said.

"Call me. I'll be discreet."

They broke the connection.

Drover stared at the receiver in his hand and tried to think of the next thing. Maybe he already knew what it was going to be. He didn't want to wade into this. This wasn't detached enough for him. He had known Fionna, even known Paul and Neil. He counted St. Mary's College among his memories of what home was like and fooled himself in lonely hotel room moments into thinking he could go home again sometime. What if he had to go home suddenly though and found out home had moved into another neighborhood and wasn't at all the way he remembered it?

He shook his head and dialed another number. One of those numbers he would never forget. The phone rang a long time and Drover hoped the number would not be answered, or be answered by someone with a Mexican accent who said the party he was calling didn't live there anymore.

"Yeah?" The gruff voice was wrinkled by sleep.

"Captain Carmody," Drover said. He tried to picture the old man. He had last seen him six years earlier, at his mother's funeral. Carmody was nearly eighty and he had the belly of a walrus and the hands of a killer. Drover could see that shape, those hands, in the voice at the other end of the line.

"Jimmy Drover," Drover said.

Another one of those pauses. People concentrate so hard on the words in a telephone call that everything said becomes a surprise that has to be gulped in. Especially at midnight on a snowy December evening in a city that is not home anymore.

"Whaddaya want, kid? You got troubles?"

"Everyone's got troubles."

"My trouble is not changing my phone number so I don't get calls from bums in the middle of the night."

"I'm not a bum yet. Still make the room rent and wear clean underwear," Drover said.

"You fucked with the vowels, you got caught."

He had said the same sort of thing at the wake of his mother. Pat Carmody was the son of immigrant Irish who grew up tough in the shadow of Little Hell, the now-vanished Italian ghetto on the near North Side. The vowels were Italians because their names ended in

31

vowels and because they were all Outfit, every pasta-eating one of them. Carmody's moral universe would make a pope feel guilty.

"I'd like to see you," Drover said. He took stuff from Carmody he wouldn't take from anyone, not even Black Kelly.

"Come by then. I was watching the movie. I must of been dozing, I thought the phone was ringing in the movie except it was a Western and John Wayne didn't have phones."

"Now?"

"You got trouble, don't you, kid?"

The voice was just as gruff but Drover could always see beneath that. He felt warm all of a sudden, as if home was still the same after all.

"Maybe."

"Take a cab. Don't ride the El at night, full of spades and spics."

"You're a lesson in tolerance."

"Tolerance is one of your California words. Real life ain't palm trees, kid."

They broke the connection.

Or maybe Drover was renewing one.

FOUR

RETIRED CHICAGO police captain Patrick Brennan Carmody lived
on the second floor of the two-flat on Cornelia Street, two miles north
from where he grew up. The Ravenswood El line down the street was
shut up for the night and there were a lot more sullen Hispanic faces
on the blocks north of Belmont and Lincoln but everything else was
the same. Cities have their own feel and Chicago always feels dark
and dangerous at night, sullen at the edges, winking and nodding and
enticing you behind the green door to see the girls. Drover noticed
the little changes. Like the kitchen chairs set in the snowy streets,
marking off parking spaces that better not be breached by gringo drivers
looking to park their wheels on a bad night. They never did that in
the old days, in the old neighborhood, in the home of Drover's memories.

Patrick Brennan Carmody wore a clean white shirt with the sleeves rolled up to expose his USMC tattoo with the eagle and the anchor of the Corps. His hair was white and short and hard, hard as his blue eyes. He needed a shave.

Drover knew whatever he was wearing himself wasn't right, was too California or too casual or too much what a bum would wear. Carmody's eyes gave that away.

Carmody stood at the door and looked at the kid for a moment and then turned and walked back to the kitchen. The place was the same, sort of a musty memory, and Carmody hadn't changed except to get incredibly older. His back was still broad and his neck thick but the skin was sagging.

There was a bottle of Early Times on the table and two glasses, one of them partly filled with brownish liquid.

"There's water in the sink," Carmody said. And sat down at the table.

The kid went to the sink, turned on the tap, got a little water, and then poured off a little of the sweetish whiskey in it.

"*Salut'*," Drover said, making a toast.

"Fuck the dago shit," Carmody said. "*Slante'*."

They had made their toasts and now they sat and stared at each other. Carmody could make his eyes harder than anything Drover had ever seen, even the eyes of the cardsharps in Vegas, even harder than the eyes of a pit boss watching the house get cheated. Carmody's eyes could be one thousand watts of the old third degree if he wanted them to be. Now they were just about two-hundred watts. Very dim.

"So what's your trouble, kid? The guineas on your ass?"

"I don't mess with the Outfit. I told you that then and I tell you that now."

"You're workin' for them."

"I free-lance for a guy named Fox Vernon. You've seen him on national TV. He's legitimate and he's as far from being an Italian as you are. He was U. of C., silver on china, his father was a big shot during the war."

"Big shots don't impress me."

"Nothing does."

"So what brings you out to Chicago on a night like this?"

34

"It was old home week. Me and my buddy. We went to see DePaul play tonight."

"Out to the Horizon?"

"They played in Alumni Hall," Drover said.

There was a flicker. Like any number of Irish kids who never had the luxury of going to college, Carmody was an unofficial alumnus of Notre Dame and also had a soft spot for the school by the El tracks, DePaul.

"They beat whoever they was playing?"

"Creighton. Clobbered them."

"Creighton was always a setup for them."

"True."

"Who's your buddy?"

"My landlord in Santa Cruz. Ex-Chicago fireman named Black Kelly. He was a captain until he broke his back."

"Probably from sleeping on it," Carmody said. He had the normal cop's dislike for firemen.

"He runs a saloon there. He came to see his relatives."

"I knew a Frank Kelly on the fire," Carmody said.

"Terrific for you."

"And who was you seein' on your old home week?"

"Nobody special. I wasn't goin' to bother you, Captain, but I thought you'd be a good place to start."

"Start with what?"

"A ref named Dan Briggs killed himself."

"I don't know him."

"But you can find out who was on the case."

"Suicide ain't much of a case."

"It gets handled, doesn't it? In homicide?"

"Why would you be interested?"

"He was a ref."

"And you're working for a bookie and you want to know why he killed himself."

Drover had an absurd need to justify himself all of a sudden. "Look, Cap, I did what I could."

"Maybe you did. The point of getting out of the gutter wasn't to go back to it when you felt like it."

35

"I was a sportswriter. A columnist. I saw someone in L.A. I knew from the old neighborhood. I talked sports crap with him for a dozen minutes. Twelve minutes. That's what they had, they had nothing. I wasn't in the Mob then, I'm not in the Mob now."

"Where there's smoke, there's an arsonist."

"Only in the warped minds of people who think suspicions are good enough."

"You don't have to hang around with them, that kind."

It had happened the way those things happen. The paper had even nominated Drover for a Pulitzer. He was as good as anyone gets in the business. And then a tinhorn U.S. attorney in Los Angeles played God and rounded up dozens of indictments on dozens of people on interstate sports gambling, including a newspaper sportswriter named Drover. The paper had dropped him right away, long before the indictment against Drover was quashed because there was no evidence he was part of any conspiracy. But suspicions always linger; the paper wouldn't hire him back; and Drover sealed his fate in the newspaper business by suing to get his old job back. He got compensation instead and he was never going to work in the sportswriting trade again. That was the truth of it but it didn't matter; once tainted, you never rub it clean again. Rumor is a bloodstain on silk.

"I hang around with whoever I want to hang with. Even ex-cops who get things wrong."

Pat Carmody's eyes glittered just then, eyes of a killer bull a moment before the charge. And then it passed. Pat Carmody tried another sip of medicine. The kitchen light was stark; the snow had softened all the sounds of the city evening.

"What do ya want, kid?"

"I knew a girl at St. Mary's, Captain. Even you'd like her. Irish girl. Except she thinks her brother's got trouble. A referee worked the Midwest Conference in the NCAA named Dan Briggs killed himself three weeks ago. Or four. He was an insurance agent on the northwest side. Had family, all that mess. He killed himself apparently after someone sent an anonymous letter to the AA board that said he was involved in a point-shaving scheme with some players. At St. Mary's. Her brother is the coach at St. Mary's."

Carmody took it in, staring at his water tumbler of whiskey and water. Then his eyes lifted heavily and he looked at Drover.

"So he killed himself out of shame."

"That's in your John Wayne Westerns, Captain. It don't happen. He had family. Insurance doesn't pay off on suicide, he'd know that."

"People make messes. I oughta know. I saw enough of that in forty-six years."

"Who'd you know in the department I could talk to?"

"So you wanna use me now for your dago friends in Vegas?"

"I want to know about a man killing himself over an anonymous letter. If there is a letter. If any of this is true."

"The Irish girl got a name?"

"Fionna Givens. She was married to Neil O'Neill who was the coach at St. Mary's until he went to ESPN."

"I don't get the cable. Costs too much. I can watch my Westerns on WGN, thank you. For free."

"The way God intended television to be."

"You never lived on a pension."

"I thought you would of stolen enough in forty-six years to get cable."

Carmody let his eyes reach eight hundred watts before dimming the lights. "A punk'd say that to me in my day would end up eating alley bricks face first."

"It'd still be true," Drover said. He was tired, maybe that explained it. Maybe he was just mad, mad at the old man here, mad at his mother for dying on him, mad because home was gone far away and could never be found again.

"You don't know a thing, kid, about the way things really are," Pat Carmody said. And it was a sad voice, Drover thought. The old man poured off some more of the cheap bourbon and didn't bother with water this time. "Your mother was a lovely woman, loveliest woman in the world aside from my own Eileen, God rest their souls." He took the drink to his lips.

"God rest their souls," Drover said. It was a true prayer and the communion wine was cheap whiskey.

"Ah," the old man said.

Silence. The kitchen clocked ticked on. The city silence smoth-
ered them. Snow and silence and two men at a kitchen table in the
back of a flat on the north side down the street from the Ravenswood El.

"I'll call Tommy Gallagher. I brought him along. He's stuck
downtown now but he's got his connections."

"I'd appreciate it. Just don't tell him a lot. Let me feel him out,
see what he knows."

"Tommy is straight, kid. He won't rat on you. No more than I
will," Carmody said. "He knows the old ways. I gotta put him on the
scene."

"I believe you then," Drover said. There was nothing else he
could say.

"Do you live all right then?"

"I got an apartment. In Santa Cruz. Up near Monterey. My
buddy and I came in to see some games. You want tickets to the Bears
game Sunday?"

"Fuck it," Carmody said. "I saw the Bears at Wrigley Field when
you could see a game close. They should of never moved out of Wrigley
Field. Soldier Field, you get tickets on the fifty yard line you're still
in the end zone. A disgrace."

"Things are," Drover agreed.

"When you called, I thought you was in trouble. You don't call,
kid."

"I'm sorry."

"Ah, it don't matter. I got my friends. Not as many but some of
us're still kicking. I don't need you. But I was missing your mother as
soon as I heard your voice and it made me sad."

Drover stared at the old man.

"You think about her?" the old man said.

"Every day. No, make that every night."

"A good woman."

"The worst part of what happened was that she believed in it. It
wasn't true but she believed in it."

The old man examined him with those large eyes. "It wasn't true,
was it, kid? Really?"

"It wasn't true," Drover said. Christ, he felt low. He realized how low he felt when he blinked and came up with wet eyes. He turned away.

"Then it was a terrible thing, what happened to you," Carmody said. Almost soft beneath the gruff, like the undergrass struggling beneath the iron weeds.

Just terrible, Drover agreed.

FIVE

Neil O'Neill had a full day in New York. There was his lawyer from ten to ten-thirty with the meter running, talking about how to get divorced from Fionna without making her a rich woman. Then there was his agent, Max Clapper, calling in from the Coast, where he was wrapping up a deal for a dumb-as-a-board arrogant basketball center from Germany named Heinrich Claus who would be the new center for the Lakers, the old center having rammed his Porsche into an oak tree in Bel Air, severing his jugular, smashing his girlfriend's skull, and decapitating the sexual organ that was in his girlfriend's mouth at the moment of impact. Max was full of good gossip like that and fed it to his new, rising TV star property Neil O'Neill almost daily. It was the purpose of the call.

Neil then worked out for an hour at the Midtown Athletic Club, running steps, doing the bicycle, lifting weights, and getting a full-court massage from Adrienne who made him hard all over.

There was lunch with Brewster Palou, who was the new owner

of the Giants football club, held in the Russian Tea Room, where more untruths and pleasantries are spilled than caviar eaten. Here Neil told the gory details of the death of the former Lakers center and his girlfriend. They had a good laugh about it and penis jokes were recalled.

The afternoon was work, or what passes for work in network television, with much bantering and some serious instruction by the director of *Doubletime,* the weekly Neil O'Neill sports commentary that occupied 22 percent of Neil O'Neill's airtime. Neil had to lose the gray at his temples, the director explained. Neil said he would do it. He was not established yet and he was still listening to the rules of the new game he found himself playing.

Finally, there was a stand-up session with Tabbi Anderson in the closed-door office on the sixth floor. She gave him all his messages, passed across correspondence to be signed and pictures to be autographed, pressed her behind against his business-suit hard-on, and let herself be penetrated while sprawled breasts-down on the rosewood desk. Work, work, work, and it was all so far removed from the pristine pomposity of St. Mary's that Neil O'Neill wondered sometimes if he had ever lived that other life.

Paul Givens, Fionna's brother, had a full day too.

"I talked to Jimmy Drover about this," Fionna said to him. It was just after eight-thirty in the morning and they were sitting in his office on the campus, the one with the leather couch, paneled walls, trophies, team pictures, St. Mary's Bulldogs pennants, and the rest of the accoutrements that speak of sports, sweat, honor, school loyalty, and the rah-rah that coaches use to intimidate visitors and friends. Lost in the wall clutter was a simple crucifix with the suffering Christ staring down at the occupants of the office. Paul was wishing he were intimidating Fionna, whose voice was clear and calm.

"You can't trust someone . . . like that."

"Who're you going to trust, Paul? You can't trust the NCAA, can you? How many times have they talked to you? They get anonymous letters and they treat them like fact."

"They don't treat them like anything except anonymous letters," Paul said. A plateful of fat doughnuts sat on the desk and he was munching. The secretaries always brought in doughnuts and it showed; the lean Paul Givens was getting a small gut.

Fionna smoked her third cigarette nervously. She was cross with Paul, cross with herself, cross with Betsy for not having the sense of a home ec major. They would never take the starry-eyed cheerleader out of Betsy who would think doughnuts made a perfectly delightful breakfast, along with Ho Hos and Ding Dongs.

"Jimmy Drover was never my friend."

"But he was mine. And you've got to get friends on your side, Paul. You're in your first season and you're doing great and what you don't need is a scandal."

"I'm not going to get a scandal." The pain lines around his green eyes belied that thought. He reached for another doughnut. "They talked to my boys, the boys talked to me."

"Is it the same guy talking to everyone?"

Paul Givens looked at the doughnuts and sighed. "He's not a dinosaur like some of them. He's got a nice manner. Went to St. John's out east."

"What's his name?"

"Cary. Cary Lucas. He's been doing investigations for the NCAA for five years. He laid it all out for me." Like most people in the college game, Paul Givens said it "N C Aaaa," spreading out the final vowel sound. Only outsiders insisted it was the N C Double A.

"What does he ask you?"

"The hard questions. Straight out. He wants to know what I know and I can get an edge to the questions by listening hard. Figure out what he means by what he asks."

"Who does he suspect?"

"I'm not going to tell you."

"You've got to tell someone."

"I talked to Father O'Brien."

"That was stupid."

"What am I going to do? They notified Father O'Brien as soon as they started the investigation. I gave him my side of it first."

"And what did Father O say?"

"He said he had complete faith in me."

"Behind you a thousand percent," Fionna said.

"Everyone isn't a liar or a double-dealer. You got bitter, Fi, Neil made you bitter."

"Neil O'Neill is an asshole," she said.

"I pray you get together with him," Paul said. His green eyes were honest bright. He probably did, Fionna thought, and her heart softened. Sweet Paul.

The team practiced at three in the rickety old gym called the House of Horrors by visiting teams. When game time came, the student body of St. Mary's cranked up, the iron rafters rattled, and the banshee sound crooned like nine thousand tuning forks in an atomic wind.

The seats were empty now. This was practice and the sounds were of lumbering feet on hardwood, squeaking soles turning on varnish, and the thump and swish of basketballs driven home. It was a good practice on a bad day, Paul thought. His heart lifted when it came down to this, the reason for everything, the core of existence. He was a lucky man and thought he knew it. When he brought the boys into the locker room at six, they said a prayer with their hands piled on each other.

"God help us every day in everything we do. Blessed Mother of God, pray for us," said the team captain, reciting the ritual by heart. His name was Albert Brown, aka the Brown Bomber, and his heart was as pure as anyone's, even if he was a Baptist. He was one helluva power forward, and when every scout and coach in the big time had beat a path to his mother's door in Pinpoint, North Carolina, to recruit him three years ago, it was considered a small miracle that he had chosen the Catholic college in the Indiana cornfields southeast of Chicago. That's what Paul Givens—then an assistant to Neil O'Neill—had thought at the time. And said so to the head coach.

Neil had grinned his now-famous grin and said, "The Lord does work in mysterious ways, Paul."

Paul had blinked at that.

"Naw. It wasn't an act of God. It was an act of common sense which Albert has to an unusual degree. I promised him the Final Four in three years and he believed me. Final Four means he goes first round into the Big Show and starts buying up cotton fields in North Carolina."

Paul wouldn't have made a promise like that. But now it looked as though it might come true in his second season as the boss of the Bulldogs.

Summer corn was dead on the stalks in the fields around St. Mary's. The campus greens were browned now, graced with oak and willow shade trees all bared now for winter. The wind was keen across the prairies. Paul walked across campus from the gym to the athletics office building. The football team had the lion's share of space there—St. Mary's Bulldogs were always a football powerhouse—but the basketball team struggled on as if football didn't matter more. It was very cold in the twilight and the walk across campus made Paul Givens feel alive. He didn't even see Father O'Brien come out of the administration building until he hailed him.

Paul stopped and waited for the priest.

Father George O'Brien—Father O to two generations of St. Mary's students and faculty—wore his clerical garb hidden by a swell tan camel hair coat and an Irish wool hat.

They walked together in silence for a moment, staring ahead in the gloom in their separate thoughts. The quaint streetlights off the quad were on and they cast small pale circles of illumination which seemed tentative as the immensity of the Indiana nightfall came over the land. There were stars in the sky and you could see them because the nearest big town was only North Fork, population 28,500.

"I was talking to Cary Lucas, just got finished talking to him on the phone," Father O'Brien said.

The perfect moment of the practice was shattered with these words. Paul felt as low as he had been accustomed to feeling all these days since the first NCAA shoe dropped.

"He was saying they want to talk some more with Albert Brown," Father O'Brien said.

"Didn't he talk to him enough the first round?"

"Take it easy, Paul. They can talk to whomever they want," Father O'Brien said.

"The Spanish Inquisition has an address in Washington, D.C.," Paul Givens said.

"Nobody expects the Spanish Inquisition," Father O'Brien said.

He gave Paul a pat on the back. Paul forced a smile. They were both secret devotees of *Monty Python's Flying Circus*, the British comedy that was in perpetual reruns on countless public television stations, and every now and then, up would pop a line from the memorized scripts. Some people would have been shocked to learn that a man like Father George O'Brien watched *Monty Python* religiously.

"You going home?" Father O'Brien said.

"I guess so," Paul said.

"You and Betsy having troubles, Paul?"

"No troubles. She went to her mother's house. It's her mom's birthday. Surprise."

"Weren't you invited?"

"I've got things to do," Paul said. He said it to shrug off the priest and Father O'Brien understood.

"I asked Cary Lucas what he suspects it was that Albert Brown did or was doing."

"What was it he said?"

"Nothing. He said it was a tangential inquiry, not based on the famous letters," Father O'Brien said.

"What the hell does that mean?"

"I put it to him but I left out the expletive," Father O'Brien said.

"And what did he say?"

"The same thing. He said he didn't want to make an allegation of any sort, not against the school or against Mr. Brown," Father O'Brien said.

"He's upset the boys," Paul said.

"I know, I know." Softly, soothing like a mother comforting a child. Another pat on the back. The wind keened on a higher note.

"Snow tonight," Father O'Brien said.

"We've got to fly out at noon tomorrow. I hope North Fork International isn't shut down," Paul said. "I've gone over the tapes on Penn State until my eyes have turned orange. We've got them even if they're playing at home."

Father O'Brien smiled. "I was thinking it was a great year. The football team gets invited to the Orange and your boys might just be in the Final Four."

"It would make recruiting a lot easier."

Father O'Brien stopped. The square face was ruddy from the night wind. "I was going to ask you about that, Paul. I wanted to have a little sit-down with you if I could. You could spare me a few minutes?"

It was framed as a question the way Father O's demands always were. Such a charmer, he could charm dollar bills off oak trees.

Paul Givens finished his day sitting with the white-haired priest in black garb in a common room in the priest's rectory near St. Mary's church on the east side of the campus. The rectory was paneled wood that smelled of lemon Pledge and old money and comfort, like a private club. Which it was in a way, a perk of priesthood.

Paul Givens took a glass of Dewar's White Label and killed it with enough soda to keep him on the straight and narrow. Father O'Brien made a manhattan, complete with a red cherry and enough bitters to cure the common cold. They settled on the leather easy chairs and watched a gas fire flicker in the fireplace and tried to imagine hobgoblins in the flames. Or at least one of them did.

"Albert is a good student. Not exceptional, he won't be any rocket scientist. But he keeps up his studies."

"They all keep up their studies," Paul said, feeling he was on the defensive all of a sudden. So much for pats on the back. "This isn't UNLV."

"No, it's not."

Thoughtful silence. But Paul wanted to stick the needle in. He wanted to make someone else hurt.

"I personally like Jerry Tarkanian. He's mostly honest, even if I don't like his methods," Paul Givens said. He had backbone beneath his gentle manner. The kids knew it; the crowds knew it; even some of the sportswriters knew it. The backbone came up when Paul was being shoved against the wall and Father O'Brien backed off a little.

"Times change, rules change. The N C Double A takes a lot of heat," Father O'Brien said. He was looking at the fire along with Paul but he was only seeing gas at twelve dollars an hour going up in smoke.

"It makes a lot of heat," Paul said. "What about Albert Brown?"

"For some reason, this Cary Lucas person is going back now three years and he wants to know how we recruited Albert Brown. This

47

comes out of the blue to me. I said he should talk to Neil O'Neill and I said we had nothing to hide, he was welcome to talk to Albert or anyone. Including you."

"Neil handled Albert Brown himself. We all conferred and I went down to the Nike camp in Indianapolis to watch him work out the summer of his junior high school year but I was just making a report to Neil."

"Did you talk to Albert?"

"You can't do that," Paul said shortly.

"Because it's against the rules."

"The rules are tricky and they change all the time but it's what I'm paid for. To keep up on the rules."

"And you made a report to Neil that Albert was a good athlete."

"I said he was a long shot for us. He was raised by his mother in Pinpoint, North Carolina. Poor and honest and God-fearing by Baptist standards, I didn't see him coming in to the Catholics," Paul said.

"But he went to a Catholic grammar school down there," Father O'Brien needled.

"I know that. But Our Lady of Grace where he went was in its last days, set up by the nuns when there were nuns plentiful enough and back when the South was segregated and only the nuns could take care of education for black kids. He got a good education but he still did his duty by God with the Pinpoint Tabernacle Baptist Church," Paul said.

"You wanted him badly enough," Father O said. He said it absently, staring at the fire.

"I wanted him. But I didn't see a way around to get him. He was going to end up going to some place like Georgetown. Georgetown or even North Carolina. Albert was good enough to get through either school and he'd play with the best. St. Mary's? What was it but a good football school? We had to fight against that."

"You resent that. I understand that. It's normal. St. Mary's is identified with football." Softly and knowingly, a wise old priest talking to the resentful kid.

The resentful kid got more so. "Yeah, I resent it. We play basketball, good basketball, but we get the short end. The glory is in football program. So's the money."

"Money? They make money for us, Paul."

"Give someone else a chance."

"Is that what you think?"

Silence.

"We graduate everyone," Paul said, veering away from the question. He didn't like the question. It implied too many things about his future. Maybe his lack of one. "We don't have slackers on the team. They study or they're out and they know it. From day one. You know that, Father."

The priest was nodding, saying nothing.

"You know that's the way Neil ran it. The way I run it. They're students first and then they're athletes."

"It's a cruel commentary, isn't it, Paul, that we have to be defensive about it?" Father O'Brien said.

Paul looked up sharply. Was he making fun of Paul? St. Mary's had been a bully pulpit in the national press for amateurizing college sports, keeping them pure. Of course, business was business and private colleges needed sports to make money. Somewhat hypocritically, the school had sabotaged a fledgling football conference three seasons earlier by withdrawing from the conference to sign a national independent contract with CBS worth $28 million. St. Mary's drew better than even *Murphy Brown*, given the time slot.

"Paul, I want you to search your mind and conscience for what happened with Albert Brown three years ago to make him sign with St. Mary's instead of one of those other schools you named."

There it was. Paul drew in his breath. "You told Cary Lucas to talk to Neil. What did Neil have to say?"

The priest got up and went to the sideboard and made another elaborate manhattan, muddling the liquid just so with juice and bitters before adding the seltzer. His back was to Paul and the fireplace.

He turned slowly and came back, stood over Paul for a moment. He said, "Neil said you handled the whole thing from beginning to end. Neil said he just took credit for signing Albert."

Paul was not aware the drink had slipped through his fingers, falling on the Oriental carpet with scarcely a sound. He was staring into the priest's eyes and they were winter.

49

"That just isn't true," Paul said. His voice was croaking. "Albert can tell him that isn't true."

"Ah, I'm sure he'll talk to Albert."

"And Albert will tell the truth."

"Will he?"

"What would he have to gain by lying?" And the silence answered Paul's question. It had been a child's question. Everything to lose by telling the truth.

"The truth. The truth is . . ." Paul hesitated. What could he say now? This man's eyes betrayed the friend; they were winter and it chilled Paul.

"I spilled my drink," he said. "I'm sorry." He bent to retrieve it. The priest didn't move. Paul looked at his polished shoe and picked up the glass.

"We all want the truth, I suppose," Father O'Brien said.

And what the hell did that mean?

SIX

Tommy Gallagher, like most cops in big cities, knew how to run up a tab when the other guy was paying. They were eating at Kiki's on north Franklin at the edge of the River North art gallery district. The place was country French bistro food and a place for conversations. Tommy had picked the place as one of the costs of Drover doing business.

Drover looked at the Xerox file for a long time while Tommy drank the first of several see-throughs, which were vermouthless martinis on the rocks. His eyes were pig-hard, asking for a fight, yet his face seemed amused at the prospect at the same time. His hair was soft red, the color of sunlight on autumn afternoons.

"I love cop-ese," Drover finally said. "Open and shut. The victim was the perpetrator."

"We can't all be Ernest Hemingway," Tommy Gallagher said. He reached across the table for the file copy. "You finished?"

"I don't get to keep it?"

"You never saw it."

Drover let the file go. Tommy tore the Xerox pages into bits and put the bits in the pocket of his sports coat.

"Captain tell you all about me?"

"Most of it. You wanna believe this Briggs guy didn't kill himself. Why is that, Jimmy? You know something we don't know?"

"I know how to write," Drover said. Something about cops put his hackles up. "I know that some anonymous letters to the NCAA aren't going to get a part-time college ref to kill himself and leave his widow and orphans widowed and orphaned."

"People kill themselves all the time. Life is hard and then they die."

"Why blow this off?"

"Number one, Jimmy, it wasn't blown off by anyone," Tommy Gallagher said. He said it mean the way he said things when he was feeling hostility, and he came down hard on the "Jimmy" just to put Drover in his place. "Number two, Jimmy, we didn't know until I talked to Carmody today that there was anything about any kind of letter sent to the N C Double A. It just gives the thing a motive as far as I can see. We might have been puzzled by why he killed himself but this ain't Agatha Christie, this is a real big city full of violent people who are always doing each other in. We got to concentrate on the real homicides, not leapers and guys who brush their teeth with shotgun shells."

"No curiosity, huh?"

"No nothing," Tommy Gallagher said. "What do your dago friends think about this?"

"What friends?"

"Carmody told me you got mixed up with the dagos in L.A., that you're working for Vegas now. I shouldn't even be seen with you except I like it when the players buy me lunch."

"I don't play," Drover said.

"Good, Jimmy. Neither do I. Like I said, what's the word on the streets—you gotta forgive my clichés, I'm not as well educated as you are—what's the word about this guy Briggs shaving points?"

"I had to start somewhere so I started with the cops. If the cops don't know, maybe nobody knows."

"Why do you think this was homicide?"

"Because it doesn't make any sense. Even with what you call a motive. The NCAA gets letters all the time from all kinds of nuts. From jealous rival coaches who want to tell you about a recruiting scandal just because they didn't get the center and some other guy did. The NCAA is a rumor factory and it feeds on greed and hypocrisy. So two and two do not make four. They might have asked a question of Dan Briggs but what kind of a question could it be for Dan Briggs to kill himself?"

"Like, 'Did you fix games?' "

"Who asked it then, Gallagher?"

That stopped him for a moment. Drover saw the hard eyes turn to the hard drink on the white tablecloth. Before he could speak, a waiter came up and they both ordered the salmon fillet. And Gallagher added a bottle of Beaujolais Villages to the running tab.

"A wine connoisseur," Drover said.

"Hell, I even subscribe to the *Condé Nast Traveler*. I try to be well rounded," Gallagher said.

"Who asked the question, Gallagher?"

"That would involve people we should have heard from, Jimmy. Was the state attorney investigating a fix? The federals? They might have thought to mention something to us when Dan Briggs messed up his rec room. Then we might have looked further. But there was nothing. *Nada.* A homicide dick named Cummings went over the thing, typed the report in language you disapprove of, and went on to other things like gang rape, murder, and combinations thereof."

"So nothing means nothing, right?"

"That's what they teach in school when they do any teaching at all," Gallagher said.

The poached salmon in dill sauce was just fine, along with the skinny carrots that still had crunch and the little boiled potatoes carved into shapes like toadstools. Drover had to admit that Gallagher was right about the wine.

"The thing is, what are you gonna do now?" Gallagher said it as slyly as he could.

"Maybe nothing."

"You come to Chicago from sunny Cal to give up because of what some dumb cop says?"

"I came to Chicago to watch the Bulls."

"I wish I had tickets to the Bulls. That's the hottest ticket in town."

"I'll get you a couple for Thursday night," Drover said.

"Fine. Send them to me at the department. I'm in Planning these days. Room four-oh-nine."

"You don't mind taking a bribe?"

"Is that a bribe, Drover, or are you doing me a favor? If it's a bribe, I might have to look at the thing differently."

Drover smiled at that. Like Carmody said, he was a straight cop and that meant different things to different people. Maybe life wasn't a TV series.

"It's a favor for a favor," Drover said.

"I already did you a favor," Gallagher said.

"I went to St. Mary's. I like the old school. I'd hate to see it get hurt."

"I went to St. Mary's too. Two years before the money ran out and I went on the department. I got no kick against St. Mary's, they played as square with me as anyone. Naturally, they gave all the blacks the scholarship money to show how fucking liberal they were, but that's the way the game is played."

"You were in sports?"

"Just not good enough to make football as a walk-on," Tommy Gallagher said.

"Nobody could walk on to their football team."

"You could if you're the right color and took the right pills."

"That's bullshit," Drover said. And they both knew it wasn't but it was part of protecting the memory of home. St. Mary's was tied into the memory. Drover thought Christmas was for real when there had been a home.

"Bullshit? Coming from you, a known consorter with known criminals?"

"I bet you consort with criminals all the time. After all, they do the crimes."

"I enjoy my work."

"I hate to see someone get set up," Drover said.

"Yeah, like you were allegedly set up in L.A. that time. I tell you, I read you when you were still in the Chicago papers. I enjoyed the hell out of what you wrote. You might say I was a fan. You shoulda never gone to the West Coast and got mixed up with people you don't want to get mixed up with."

"Stayed pristine in Chicago, well-known center of good government and low crime rates."

"At least you know the streets here," Gallagher said. He was the kind who never let it go, never backed down from an insult or repartee, who grabbed like a bulldog and bit to the bone. Drover found himself admiring him without trusting him. Maybe it was the wine. The wine had been a good choice from a suprising source. Cops were never what they seemed. Play acting was part of their lives.

"Look, talk to someone at the state's attorney's office, will you? Just look into it—"

"I won't go near the place. For what? For you? To fuck up a good dick like Cummings who filed an honest report? Fuck you, Drover. I owe Carmody going back and that's why I'm breathing the same air as you, but don't think we're fellow alumni from St. Mary's or I give a rat's ass if some sleaze fixed games. I don't even like basketball."

"You like the Bulls," Drover said.

"What? You doing me a big favor? Fuck your tickets, friend, I don't go down on anyone."

"Does Paul Givens?" A moment of silence.

"I knew him. A little. He was a prissy bastard, made the sign of the cross before every free throw like a fucking Puerto Rican. I got no feeling for him."

"What about Fionna? His sister?"

Wild shot. Sometimes they bring down the buck.

"What about her?"

"She asked me. Didn't the captain tell you that?"

"You know the captain never sullies a woman's name. Unless she's a whore."

"Fionna called me in, not whoever you think I work for in Vegas, which I don't," Drover said. "You knew her."

"Shit, I loved her."

"We were on campus the same time, why didn't I know you?"

"I wasn't on campus."

Drover stared at him.

"I lived over a tavern in North Fork. I paid thirty-five dollars a month and worked the weekend bar. I was twenty-two when I tried college, I didn't have the money but they gave me a wink and a nod and they said I could try to work it out. I ate peanut butter for breakfast, lunch, and supper."

"Saved the cost of board."

"Saved everything I could. I didn't have a sponsor."

"No wonder the captain took you over. He was always looking for projects. Funny, you never think of Carmody as a saint in sheep's clothing."

Gallagher was struck silent. The buzz of conversation around the room was background music to their thoughts.

"You dated her?" Drover said.

"I tried. She was very nice and I think I was too rough for her. I mean, I was out of Nam and girls were things and I fucked it up from the get-go. But she was nice to me. I probably broke my heart over her. She was something to you." Not a question.

"I was in love. Everyone was in love with Fionna."

"Yeah, I was on the list. But it wasn't going to work out. She called you, huh? You must have been special."

"She called me because she needs something. Someone. To clear the air gathering around her brother. She's doing it for Paul."

"And Paul is a name that might be part of some point-shaving scandal."

"She thinks so."

"What do you think?"

"I guess I lose my belief in saints and then you remind me that there must be good people left someplace. I don't know. I can't even see Paul figuring out how to set up a fix, let alone do it."

"Neither do I."

"But his name was on a letter sent to the NCAA."

"Some jealous coach, like you said earlier."

"Maybe. I was just grasping at straws, Gallagher. I just wanted to see if I could make a mattress or start a fire. I saw Fionna last night for the first time in fifteen years and she looked haunted by this and I wanted to tell her it was going to be all right."

Something had broken down between them with the mention of Fionna Givens. Something was shared now, some common memory that swept away the intervening years and the natural hostility between them.

"Whaddaya gonna do now?" the cop said.

"Find out who's running the investigation for the NCAA, I guess. He won't talk to me but I'll give it a try."

"He won't talk to you because you're tainted."

"That's what the D.A. in L.A. said. He wasn't right but there it is."

"It's like original sin only you can't baptize it away," Gallagher said. "You keep carrying the stain."

The remark was so profound to Drover that he just sat and stared at the cop with pig-hard eyes.

"Who were you gonna talk to?"

"Talk around. Sportswriters are a club. I got friends. Try to shake the tree for just one apple without bringing all the apples down."

"Naw," Tommy Gallagher said all of a sudden. He looked at Drover and then glanced down to see if there was anything left on his plate. "Lemme talk around first."

"Talk to who?"

"Guys. I know more guys than you do. In this town, anyway. Where you staying?"

"Drake."

"Yeah, okay. Maybe I'll call you."

"When would that be?"

"Maybe tomorrow. Maybe around three in the afternoon. I got some people I can talk to."

"About what?"

"About Dan Briggs and why he killed himself," Gallagher said.

"Detective Cummings."

"I can do that but I don't want to. I want to keep this easy. I know guys."

And Drover was sure he did.

SEVEN

BLACK KELLY detached himself from his firemen buddies at the end of the bar and joined Drover at the front. The plate glass window of Maguire's on Webster Avenue showed a street muddy with blackened snowdrifts and a row of parked cars that wouldn't be going anywhere soon. Three inches had fallen overnight and the snow mired the city in gloom: This was only December and winter was a long stretch coming. The Howard Street elevated line spanned the street fifty feet east of Maguire's and it was the habit to suspend conversations in midsentence when the El train rumbled by.

"How's old home week coming?" Drover said.

"You get any satisfaction from the cop?"

"Not really."

"I didn't think you would. Cops are the last place to turn for information," Black Kelly said. He was smiling and his very blue eyes were merry, a kid with a secret.

"So I beat another bush. I have to find out what the NCAA knows and when they knew it," Drover said. He had been thinking about how to do it all afternoon.

"I was talking to Ted Lewandowski, was an engineer over at Third Battalion when I was there, a helluva nice guy," Kelly began.

Drover waited through the preamble. A Black Kelly story was coming. It would have entrances and exits and characters out of Shakespeare, all leading to an inevitable punch line that might—or might not—be germane to the beginning. There was a ritual to Kelly's stories, and getting to the punch line was not as important as the trip along the way. The bartender came down the boards and Kelly made a swizzle motion with his finger. "V.O. and soda, a child's portion," he said.

"Diet whatever," Drover said.

"This must be serious," Kelly said.

"I drank wine for lunch. I hate drinking wine for lunch. It puts me in a beddy-bye mood."

"Ted Lewandowski hangs out on Irving Park Road in a place called Glasses," Kelly said, shortening the story somewhat, though Drover didn't know that.

"Nice name," Drover said.

"Glasses has this book named Leo Myers," Kelly said.

"All right, Plato, what question do I ask next?"

"Leo Myers has a big customer or had one up till a couple of weeks ago. Very heavy player."

Drover took a sip of the diet whatever and let the ersatz sweetness roll across his tongue. He stared at Kelly. "Dan Briggs."

"Do you suppose it's ethical for a college ref to bet on sports?"

"I'm sure the NCAA has a rule on it somewhere," Drover said.

"Ted knew Dan slightly from the bar. From Glasses. I told you it was on Irving Park Road?"

"You told me," Drover said.

"He put a bet down now and then with Leo Myers, nothing strenuous, just to make watching the games on Sunday interesting."

"Football bettor."

"Who doesn't?"

"Was Dan into Leo? Did Ted Lewandowski know?"

"Everyone knows everything," Black Kelly said. It was the setup to a lecture. "But nobody knows nothing when it comes down to it. If I had pushed it along that maybe Dan Briggs owed a lot of money to Leo Myers, then he would have said he heard that. He doesn't know. Besides, it sounds like Leo Myers is just a two-joint bookie, very small time."

"The smaller they are, the meaner they can get," Drover said.

"You think this Leo Myers arranged to hit Dan Briggs? Or pushed him into committing suicide?"

"Bookies don't collect from dead clients," Drover said. "But you don't know how deep is deep until you're in it up to your chin."

"Or over your head."

"Maybe I should ask him," Drover said. "What's he look like?"

"I didn't go into it too close. That's Ted's joint, not mine. I didn't want my name getting spread around because I was overly interested in Dan Briggs killing himself," Kelly said.

"It's a wise man who knows when to go anonymous," Drover said. The diet drink was doing it, cutting the cobwebs off and polishing his taste buds. "Maybe I should just go over to Glasses and cut the cards."

"That's the direct and brutal way," Kelly said.

"What do you suggest?"

Kelly shrugged his big shoulders. "I dunno. I'm thinking about going back to Santa Cruz. The old pier never looked more tempting than it does after three inches of premature snow in Chicago. I lived in cold weather all my life. I fought in fires when I couldn't move my fingers without breaking icicles."

"You've let your blood thin out," Drover said.

"Besides, my sister cooks like an Irishwoman," Kelly said.

"Is that bad?"

"Why do you think all the Irish kids became firemen? So we could cook for ourselves once every three days," Kelly said. "I won't leave you in the lurch if you need me—"

"Naw. I'm going through the motions for an old girlfriend, that's all. I think the suicide thing sounds bogus but the cops don't and they count. I'll ask a few more questions and join you in a couple of days."

"We can go up to Carmel for a couple of days, hang out in Clint Eastwood's saloon now that the tourist season is over," Kelly said.

"You just want to be in his movies," Drover said.

"I can act better than Sondra Locke."

"But you're only half as pretty."

Drover took a cab to the saloon on Irving Park Road a couple of blocks east of Kedzie. It was a typical Chicago street corner saloon with a large Old Style beer sign hanging over the sidewalk, small windows festooned with curtains, and a sign on the door that said NO MINORS ALLOWED.

The inside was tavern dark. A big Bears poster from a beer company rested above the back bar and showed the remainder of the football schedule. The Bears would make the play-offs again and figure out how to lose by the second game. The big question as always was who should be quarterback. The Bears hadn't had a quarterback since Sid Luckman and the T formation in the forties.

Drover slid on a stool and ordered a Red Label on the rocks with a seltzer back. The Red Label bottle had a coat of dust on it, indicating it didn't get much call in this place and that the housekeeping was not overly fastidious in any case. The barman squinted at him as in invitation to conversation but Drover wasn't feeling talkative.

It took him all of ten minutes to figure out that the guy monopolizing the pay phone at the back of the tavern was the bookie. Leo Myers was small, dark, and ugly. He had big ears and a worried look to his pale amber eyes. Drover checked him out at closer range by going to the bathroom marked GUYS. The other one was called DOLLS. Glasses was a real swinging place and the paper towel dispenser was broken.

They were watching *Jeopardy* on the box over the bar and making bets on the answers. A half-dozen people with the afternoon lonelies were making noise and the bartender, wearing a short-sleeved polo shirt, was working on improving his potbelly with a glass of Old Style.

Leo finally, almost reluctantly, hung up and headed back to the bar. He was two stools north of Drover which was close enough to ask a question.

"Was Dan Briggs into you for much?"

Leo Myers turned to Drover. His face was drained pure white.

But this was no rabbit. The half smile on Leo's ugly mug stayed right where it was.

"Do I know you?"

"You're going to," Drover said. He put his eyes into Cop Look Number Two, the cop look that isn't hostile yet unless you want to push it in that direction.

"Then give yourself a name."

"Leo," Drover began in the cop way of talking, "My name is Drover and I'm with the NCAA."

"What do you do for them?"

"I ask questions. I been asking questions about Dan Briggs."

"I know a Dan Briggs comes in here."

"Since his recent suicide? That's one hell of a trick."

"Oh yeah. I mean, I heard he killed himself. Too bad. Maybe he was sick."

"Leo, I don't want to pull teeth or give you a headache. I want to know if Dan Briggs was into you."

"You mean I loaned him money? Naw."

"I mean, you little shit, your book. You gonna say you ain't a book? Then I'll call my buddy Tommy Gallagher downtown and he'll throw you in with animals for a pleasant week at the jail."

"Who's Tommy Gallagher?"

"Lieutenant Gallagher to you. CPD."

"You got some identification or something?"

"Or something," Drover said. He pulled out the card imprinted with the logo of the NCAA board of governors, complete with his own photo and an impressive seal. He had about twenty of these cards making him a San Francisco police inspector, a special agent for the FBI, an investigator for the Internal Revenue Service, and other roles he played in life. Cards impressed people.

Leo turned the card over in his hands a few times. Drover thought he might bite it to see if it was real. When he handed the card back, the manner of the book had changed.

"You were investigating Briggs, huh?"

"Exactly. We got a little birdie whistling he might have been involved in games. Making games go a little this way or that."

"I ain't involved in that stuff. I don't want no trouble. I'm a little guy," Leo Myers said.

"You should have drunk your milk when you were a kid, maybe you'd have been a big guy," Drover said.

"Look, what do you want me to tell you?"

"I want to know about Dan Briggs. It's against NCAA regulation 489.2 for any official, referee, umpire, employee, university administrator, faculty, or player to bet or to be seen in the company of known bettors of any game, sport . . ."

"Save it," Leo said. "Whaddaya gonna do to him now? He's dead. As in dead."

"We want to know why."

"Beats me."

The bartender had been edging closer to them to pick up the conversation. Drover looked up sharply. "You wanna get me another and get Leo here one and then go down to the other end of the bar and watch *Jeopardy!*"

The barman with the belly glared at him but poured off two more drinks. Leo was into Early Times and water, just like Captain Carmody. Cops and crooks drink alike, Drover thought, scooping back his change from a sawbuck.

Leo drank without acknowledging the freebie.

"Was he a heavy hitter?"

"Anything I tell you gets me into trouble," Leo Myers said.

"Why? You don't work for the NCAA."

"You already rattled my cage with the name of your pal downtown. Gallagher or whatever the hell his name is."

"I did it to get your attention." Drover switched to Cop Look Number Four. This one is mild, us-against-them, we're-all-in-this-together, let's-be-pals. If Leo noticed the change, it didn't register on his sneer.

"I don't know what you mean by a heavy hitter."

"What kind of car did he drive?"

"Kind of car? What kind of question is that?"

"I'm trying to figure the guy out."

"Caddy. Couple of years old. Lots of guys have Caddys."

"He lived in Sauganash."

"Naturally. Nice house, I guess. I was never invited. We just did business."

"He write you insurance?"

"As a matter of fact, he did. My car insurance. I had to buy it from someone, might as well buy it from a customer."

"What did he bet on, Leo?"

"Football."

"Football?"

"Football. Pro games. Never college games."

"And never basketball?"

"Never basketball," Leo said. Staring steadily.

"I don't believe that."

"Then go fuck yourself, I give a shit what you believe."

"But you do, Leo. If I don't believe your answers, it gets complicated."

"Look, anything I say to you is against me—"

"I already know that Dan Briggs bet with you. You're a book. I know more than I knew this morning."

"Look. Tell you the truth, I don't get action in college basketball. Football, yeah. Guys come in here are football nuts. Basketball, you get basketball in the yuppie parts of town. Go down there to ask questions. Lincoln Park. Streeterville. The sophisticated crowd. Look, when the Bulls were winning the championship, I finally got a little action in basketball. Chump action, betting on the Bulls no matter what. Hometown bets. That's all. These guys don't follow college basketball. Hell, what kind of football do they bet except Nortre Dame? See what I mean?"

It sounded honest enough to be true. Drover stared at Leo for a moment and then picked up his drink. "I see what you mean," Drover said.

That warmed it up a little.

Leo remembered his manners and raised his glass. "Cheers," he said. He took a sip. "I wouldn't figure Dan Briggs to fix games. I just wouldn't figure it. He saved me a fortune on auto insurance."

Drover thought about that.

"I mean, the guy was a regular guy. Had to hustle for a buck like anyone. If he bet on football, he was close to the vest. He did a little of this and that. Figured the spread and came in on Thursday with his picks, after the injury reports. Sometimes he won and sometimes he lost, you know how it goes. He liked football."

"But he was a college basketball ref."

"So if he was betting on games, everyone in here would know it and then what would happen. Someone would tell someone or send a note to you guys and then you'd bounce him faster than a third-party check."

Drover was thinking the same thing.

"Look, you got a number or something, someplace I can reach you? I hear anything, I'll call you," Leo said.

"Sure you will," Drover said.

"Hey, I got nothing to hide."

"Was Dan sick or something? Did he seem worried about something?"

That glaze came over the amber eyes of the bookie. Drover knew the glaze was the first stage of lying for some people. It put them in the mood to lie.

"He was the same one day to the next, to tell you the truth. He came in, had a couple of beers, sometimes he killed a slow afternoon here. He studied the spreads and talked a good football game. He was smart about football."

What was the lie? Drover knew it was there now, buried in the words.

"Where else did he hang out?"

Leo looked away, back to his drink. "I wasn't his best buddy, you know. I didn't spend Thanksgiving dinner with him, you know."

"He didn't have Thanksgiving dinner this year," Drover said.

"Yeah. I don't know why a guy gives up on himself and that's the truth. I just know him as a guy who came in here and put down some bets on football games, that's all I know. Just a guy."

"I'm staying at the Drake Hotel for the time being. Room six-oh-nine," Drover said. "You can call me there if you want."

"Sure, sure," Leo said. It was ridiculous. Leo was straining to break the thing off and it showed.

"You gonna call me?" Drover said. A thin smile formed on his lips.

"If I get something, I give you a call," Leo said.

"Yeah." It was really hopeless and Drover felt drained. He would tell Fionna that he had to go to California and good luck to her and . . .

"Yeah," Drover said again, dropping a buck on the bar. He got up and looked again at Leo and turned. He wondered if Leo would palm the buck before the bartender saw it.

EIGHT

TWO MESSAGES were waiting for Drover at the hotel. He dialed the first number and hummed while the phone rang.

Lieutenant Gallagher," the voice said.

"Drover."

"You son of a bitch." Flat, like a statement of fact. "I want to see you."

"Why?"

"Because I ask around and I get answers I didn't want."

"Where should I meet you?"

"Is it cocktail hour yet?"

Drover didn't say anything.

"You still got an expense account?"

"Visa is still extending credit."

"Downstairs in a half hour in the Coq d'Or," Gallagher said. "I like those executive drinks."

"At seven bucks a pop, they're a bargain," Drover said.

"I'm expensive but I'm good," Gallagher said. He broke the connection.

Drover stared at the phone, at the nightstand next to the bed, at the number listed on the second message. It was long-distance. He knew the area code; he had gone to college in that area code.

Fionna must have been waiting all afternoon by the phone. She picked it up on the first ring.

Fionna Givens sounded grave, on the edge of panic but holding it down.

"I talked to Paul. Something's happened and he won't tell me. He had a talk with Father O, he said I should stay out of this and that you should go back to California—"

"He said I should crawl back under the rock I came out of," Drover said.

"Something like that. But this is different. I saw him yesterday, he was upset, but this morning, he was really upset, something bad had happened. I asked him what it was and he said he'd had a little talk with Father O last night and then he decided he didn't want to tell me anything. But he does. It's about to burst . . . "

"Where is he?"

"They play Penn State tomorrow night. They flew out this afternoon."

"When's he back?"

"Tomorrow night after the game. They've got a charter," she said.

"You talked to him, he give you any names, anyone investigating for NCAA?"

"A man named Cary Lucas."

"Cary Lucas. Anyone he's zeroing in on?"

"He talked to the whole team, one by one. Paul didn't say anyone in particular."

Silence.

"Can you talk to his wife?"

"Why? If he wouldn't tell me, he wouldn't tell her."

"It's his wife, Fionna. Men talk to their wives sometimes."

"Not Betsy. Not about things like this. Betsy is in a dreamworld," Fionna said. Said with contempt. Or was it jealousy? The thought bothered Drover.

"Give her a wake-up call."

"Paul would be upset."

"You already said he's upset. Look, Fionna, I don't have anything you didn't already give me. I'm rattling cages, walking around, but I don't have anything."

"About Briggs? About killing himself? I thought about what you said, about him not killing himself."

"Don't think about that now. Think about seeing Betsy and trying to find out what Paul is worried about now."

Silence. Drover could almost see her, see the stubborn set of her pretty jaw. "I can try," she said in a short burst.

"Give it a try. What is this number?" Drover said.

"I'm in a Motel Six in North Fork."

"I got to see a man in a half hour, I'll call you back tonight," Drover said.

"I don't know how to talk to Betsy," she said.

"Tell her the truth. Nobody is that isolated," Drover said.

"You don't know her."

"Try, Fionna," Drover said.

They broke the connection.

Tommy Gallagher sipped the beginning of his third martini of the day. Drover sat across from him in the clubby, wood-paneled room off the main entrance of the venerable old hotel and dipped his hand into the silver-plated peanut bowl.

"Dan Briggs was carrying cargo," Tommy Gallagher said.

"Like what?"

"He had maybe fifty or sixty policies set through Midwest Mutual. The insurance outfit that collapsed last summer. You read about it?"

"I never get beyond the sports pages."

"I didn't want to know all this. It muddies up a nice tidy little suicide. Not that it makes it something else, it just gives a motive for killing himself. He lost a lot of business when Midwest was seized by the insurance regulators. Lots of angry customers. Lots. That's what I got."

"How'd you get that?" Drover said, thinking of Leo Myers the bookie. The bookie had said that nothing was changed in Dan Briggs's life. Liar, liar, pants on fire.

"I broke my word, I called Cummings, the dick who handled the case. He said he had thought about it after filing the report, he had sniffed around and when he found a motive, he felt better about it."

"A motive for Dan Briggs to kill himself."

"Business went south when the big insurance company collapsed and Dan Briggs was hurting bad."

"So he killed himself and arranged it in such a way that everyone would know it was suicide and whatever insurance he carried wouldn't go to his kid," Drover said.

Tommy Gallagher looked wise at him. "You annoy me, Drover."

"Wait till I do my Jackie Mason impression, you want to see major annoyance," Drover said.

"You want this to be something it isn't," Gallagher said.

Drover picked up his scotch and tried it. It tasted good. "I want you to quit bullshitting me. You didn't run over here to share the news that Dan Briggs really did commit suicide."

"See, it was his shotgun. He had it from his father. Sat over the fireplace in the basement rec room. But he never hunted, never shot. Just had this old piece and Cummings said he must have gone out and bought shells for it."

"Terrific," Drover said.

Gallagher made a face. "You don't believe this, do you?"

"No," Drover said.

"What makes you so smart?"

"I finished college, remember? I'm at least two years up on you."

"Asshole."

"Perfect," Drover said. "I know Dan Briggs's name comes up in an anonymous report to the NCAA. I know he kills himself shortly thereafter and writes out a suicide note. I now he kills himself in a strange, messy way for a guy who just happens to have his daddy's old shotgun but has never used it himself. He goes out to some anonymous ammo store and buys shells, goes home, writes a note, and then blows his head off. Very awkward way of killing yourself."

"Hemingway did it like that," Gallagher said.

"You must have been an English major." Forget admiring the guy for picking good wine. A cop was a cop.

"You got a hard-on for cops. Must of picked it up from your dago friends in Vegas."

"I want to know what you really think," Drover said, ignoring it.

Gallagher bit his lip and then picked up his see-through. The dim light caught the glow in the ice cubes. "I really think that I'd like to know what the NCAA connection is to all this."

"So would I."

"You got a name?"

"Got a name named Cary Lucas, he's an investigator for the board of governors. He's looking into charges against St. Mary's basketball program."

"And he's the connection to Briggs."

"I'm assuming that. It's a big assumption but it's a place to start," Drover said.

"Remind me again, Drover. You're doing all this for some girl you used to go to school with?"

"Fionna asked me. I was in town and it didn't seem that hard. You never do a favor for anyone?"

"When I have to."

"I work for Fox Vernon part-time. He's a bookmaker in Vegas and he sets lines. He is legal and not in the Outfit, not that he doesn't know some of those guys. Fox Vernon hires me sometimes to ghost-write books for him and sometimes he hires me to watch games and tell him what I think of how they're played. A book does not want a crooked line anywhere. It's in his interest that I find out what I can about St. Mary's and about zebras who might be kinky," Drover said. "But the captain told you about me already, right?"

Gallagher nodded. "All right. That's more like it. I distrust someone doing something for the sake of auld lang syne. All right."

"I'm glad I passed inspection," Drover said.

"You do the obvious thing?" Gallagher said.

"I must not have," Drover said.

Gallagher smiled. "Wouldn't it be obvious to see what games Briggs reffed the last year or two? Couldn't your bookie friend in Vegas do that and check out the spread? I mean, if Briggs was calling fouls to shave points on a game, wouldn't someone somewhere have a record of it?"

Drover stared right at him hard to hide his embarrassment. It was the obvious thing—and Drover hadn't thought of it. Then he shrugged, making a lie: "I already made that call. I should hear back tonight."

"Is that right? You thought of it, huh? Bullshit but let it go. You give me some angle on Briggs and I'll look at it."

Drover was thinking about Tommy Gallagher. There was an urgent sense of street smarts hidden behind the cool, cynical façade. Maybe he didn't have any choice.

"There's a book works out of a saloon on Irving Park Road called Glasses. Name is Leo Myers."

"So?"

"One of his customers was Dan Briggs," Drover said.

"Briggs was a bettor? I thought you weren't supposed to do that when you were reffing games."

"Leo says Briggs only bet football. How the hell do I know what Briggs bet? I can't beat it out of Leo."

"But I can? Is that it?"

"You can show him your junior Dick Tracy badge and impress him. I dropped your name on him, so you won't have to overintroduce yourself."

Gallagher flushed then. "Where the hell do you get off using my name?"

"I've got chutzpah," Drover said. "He's a little guy born with a sneer on his face and he's always using the pay phone."

"How'd you run across him?"

"I know people too. It's a big town," Drover said.

"Maybe I'll talk to Leo Myers."

"Maybe you can see what Leo's connection is. I mean, he's paying street tax to someone to stay in business."

"I know how it works, Drover," Tommy Gallagher said.

"I didn't have any doubts about that."

NINE

THE ST. Mary's Bulldogs were suited up in the gymnasium in Pennsylvania, getting ready for the game against the Nittany Lions. It was raining in Pennsylvania. Back home in Indiana it was snowing.

Dave Zekman was driving a Buick this year, given a deep discount at Boxman Buick in North Fork because he was who he was—athletic director of St. Mary's College and the Man Who Was Going To Change Things. He was plowing through the unplowed narrow road that led across the campus to the residence of the priest faculty. The radio was picking up the pregame chatter of the longtime "voices" of St. Mary's college basketball.

They'd go next, Dave Zekman thought to himself. He was a narrow-bodied man who favored sharp black business suits and a weekly manicure at the beauty shop in North Fork. His appearance was fastidious. He brushed his black hair straight back from his squarish forehead, enhancing the deepness of his brown eyes and the cadaverous hollows of his cheeks. And he was Father O's number one boy, given the complex charge of squeezing as much profit as possible out of the athletic program.

He had to proceed carefully. The football program could be tinkered with to maximize profit—only if the right man was coach. The old coach had been John Waters, a likable, decent man who had picked up two national championships in fifteen years. Not bad but not good enough. The new coach was in the Orange Bowl in his second year and would be number one in the AP poll next season. That record had led to a sudden $28 million exclusive contract with one of the television networks that would increase St. Mary's coast-to-coast exposure and make money hand over fist at the same time.

Father George O'Brien came down the steps and slipped into the passenger seat. The two men exchanged pale smiles and they spoke each other's first names.

The Buick Park Avenue—an obscenely expensive vehicle masquerading as less than a Cadillac—crunched through the snow like a tank. They both listened to the "voices" of St. Mary's.

"Red is losing it. He misidentifies half the players, keeps calling Polanski 'Polski,' " Dave Zekman thought to say.

Father O'Brien frowned. Personnel matters were never easy. There were old friends in too many high places, and sentiment was no excuse for not helping St. Mary's prepare for real life in the twenty-first century. Those were things Father O said to himself when he began to have second thoughts about some of the things they were doing.

"Red had a good run at it," Father O'Brien said.

"Exactly. Twenty-one years on the air. I'm going to talk to him right after the Final Four, I think we can work something out that will satisfy you," Dave Zekman said. "There's a good voice in Cincinnati right now, I think he'd be right for us next season. If there is a next season."

"A St. Mary's grad?"

"No, I don't believe so."

Silence. The awesome Indiana night, fierce and black and bleak, enveloped the car and the passengers and the old voice on the radio.

"If there is a next season," Father O'Brien said, repeating Dave Zekman's words.

"I spoke with Cary Lucas again. He's going down to North Carolina, he wants to talk to Albert Brown's family," Dave Zekman said.

"Paul Givens. I talked to Paul last night, wanted to see if he had anything to tell me," Father O'Brien said. "He keeps insisting that Neil handled the recruitment of Albert Brown."

"Albert seems confused. That's what Cary Lucas said. If Cary brings up Paul Givens's name, then Albert talks about him; if he brings up Neil O'Neill's name, Albert talks about him as if he was the main man. Albert is eager to please but it doesn't make it any easier for us, for Cary Lucas—"

"Who did it to us? That's what I would love to know, who had it in for us," Father O'Brien said, his bleak eyes surveying the snowscape.

"There's a lot of envy, Father. St. Mary's is seen riding too high. You know that. The St. Mary's mystique is what they call it," Dave Zekman said.

"I've known Paul Givens as a student and as a player and now as coach. I swear Paul Givens wouldn't be doing anything illegal," Father O'Brien said.

Dave Zekman was very cool now. They were approaching the lights of North Fork. They had dinner in the same place, sometimes once or twice a month, sometimes more often. It was a small Italian restaurant and their table was in the back and students rarely went there because it was quiet and too expensive.

"But you wouldn't say the same for Neil O'Neill, and Paul worked for Neil for four seasons," Dave Zekman said. It had been a sore point, one of several between Father O'Brien and Zekman. Zekman had wanted to get rid of the whole structure set up by Neil O'Neill, including his assistant coach and heir apparent, Paul Givens. It was all too cosy, Zekman had argued, Neil was married to Givens's sister, it was practically as though they treated the basketball program as their private preserve. In the end, Father O'Brien had endorsed Paul over Zekman's desire to execute a nationwide search for a new basketball coach. Zekman had nearly quit then, but in his cool way, he waited out his anger.

"I wouldn't say a word against Neil O'Neill," Father O'Brien said. "Except that I think he treated Fionna shamefully after he went into

77

television. Paul said Fionna thinks Neil is going to file for divorce as soon as he can figure out a way not to pay her alimony."

The streets of North Fork were bright orange under the glare of the anticrime lamps. The snow was deep and plow trucks were rumbling up the main drags, burying cars and curbs in snowdrifts taller than a man.

They parked in the plowed lot in front of the Trattoria Gambini. There weren't many customers.

They sat in the back, under the mural of Firenze, and ordered drinks. When the drinks came, they let them sit there for a moment, each lost in separate thoughts.

"If it's a recruiting violation, what does that do to us?"

"I think we confess it," Dave Zekman said. "I think we give Paul Givens a chance to resign and maybe we accept a suspension from postseason play for a year. That won't kill us. It gives us the chance to look around for a supercoach and see if we can fashion a new contract. I want national television in five years, max. We won't get what we got on the football because St. Mary's and football are one and the same, but I think we can generate some genuine enthusiasm for basketball if we take a whole new look at the program."

Father O'Brien picked up his manhattan. He was troubled, and it showed in his rheumy eyes. "I just don't think Paul Givens would do anything illegal. He's a good man, a fine father."

"I didn't say he did anything illegal. What's illegal? You got John Thompson at Georgetown gets two hundred thousand a year from Nike shoes to consult. Consult about what? You know and I know that money is driving basketball from the high schools on up and it's shoe money, Nike, Reebok, Converse, all of them. We stand above that and what do we get for it? We get an N C Double A investigation saying, among other things, that a referee who went to school at St. Mary's killed himself and was named in an anonymous letter as fixing games. Dan Briggs."

"Dan Briggs, God rest his soul," Father O'Brien said, making the sign of the cross.

"God rest his soul," Dave Zekman said, picking up his martini. "I can't believe he killed himself."

"Well, he did and that's that. I hate to say this, Father, you know

I do, but the basketball program smells to high heaven. The N C Double A isn't investigating just because it likes to investigate things."

"I remember when Neil O'Neill announced Albert Brown was coming to us, I couldn't believe the news myself," Father O'Brien said.

"Too good to be true," Dave Zekman said. The words were left there, quiet and spaced apart, empty as the worry in the old priest's eyes.

"So it may be. What's the worst they could do?"

"They could give us the death penalty—cancel the season—but they won't do that. This is the first serious allegation against St. Mary's ever. They'll slap our wrists and tell us to behave and I think we have to be ready then to talk to Paul about giving up the team."

"And put him on faculty."

"On faculty," Dave Zekman said.

"But what about this point-shaving thing, with Dan Briggs?" Father O'Brien said.

"They aren't going to go into that too deeply. After all, the N C Double A doesn't want to draw attention to itself by suggesting the zebras might be bribable. And besides, Dan Briggs is dead," Zekman said. It was a little too cold for Father O'Brien's taste. His eyes looked offended. His jaw became set in stone the way the Irish show displeasure.

"If Albert got into a recruiting problem, we can live with that," Zekman said.

"But what about the boy?"

"Albert might or might not be burned, it depends on who did what to whom for what. I can see this Cary Lucas focusing on that now. Maybe someone gave Albert's mother secret money and she persuaded Albert to go to St. Mary's. Maybe it was something else. Albert doesn't have to be the tainted one. He's a sweet young man but he's not going to find the cure for cancer or split the atom," Zekman said.

"There's too much money, all of it. I sometimes wonder what would happen if we just stopped having college sports, just get out of the business," Father O'Brien said.

"Hutchins did that at the University of Chicago," Dave Zekman said, picking up a menu. He studied it for a moment and then looked across the checkered tablecloth to the priest. "But we're not the University of Chicago, not even close to it."

"We're a decent school," Father O'Brien said.

Dave Zekman waited.

"I just hate the idea of all the money, the corruption, and the temptation of young men," Father O'Brien said.

"I told you when you brought me here," Dave Zekman said.

The priest looked up.

"Athletics is the money machine. We make money providing entertainment and we use it for good. For scholarships and salaries, buildings and labs, and all the rest of it. If you're going to have athletics, then make a buck on it. We aren't even close to making the top buck on basketball, not like we're doing in football. A buck, Father, is a buck. It doesn't grow on trees, you got to work for it. That's what you hired me for and that's what I'm trying to do."

Yes, that's what he had hired Zekman for. Exactly.

TEN

FOX VERNON got back to him in forty minutes. It was amazing what Fox Vernon could do with computers.

The phone rang in the hotel room on the sixth floor of the Drake Hotel. Drover stepped naked out of the shower, wrapped a towel around his middle, and went into the bedroom to answer it. The walls were lined with bookcase façades that resembled books if books were really seven eights of an inch deep and made of fiberboard.

"Well, it is interesting. Dan Briggs reffed three games last season involving St. Mary's, and the results beat the spread every time. In fact, of twenty-five games last year, Dan Briggs and his fellow zebras were referee to seventeen games that beat the conventional line," Fox Vernon said. He was so connected in the world of statistics and computer retrieval he could probably tell exactly how many angels did dance last year on the head of a pin.

"I don't like that, Foxy," Drover said. "It makes it look like Dan

Briggs was in pretty deep and maybe all those names turned into the NCAA mean something after all."

"Reality has its unpleasant side," Fox Vernon said. "The spread on St. Mary's is plus four against Penn State tonight."

"Kind of early in the season to have that big a spread," Drover said. "Or am I wrong?"

"You're learning the Vegas way of thinking," Fox Vernon said. There was nearly a smile in his voice. "It is early, but the conventional is that St. Mary's will steamroller this season, maybe go twenty-eight-and-oh before the play-offs."

"I saw them play, they're human. The Polish kid is streaky and Albert Brown gets fooled sometimes."

"And you were telling me they were going all the way," Fox Vernon said.

"I believe that too. But not unbeaten. Not with their schedule."

"Anyway, you getting any closer to finding out what the NCAA knows?"

"A little," Drover lied.

"You want to share?"

"Briggs was into a local bookie, I don't know how deep, I got a man on it," Drover said.

"What kind of a man?"

"Dick Tracy type," Drover said.

"Why would a cop do you a favor?"

"Why not? I pay taxes."

"Just asking," Fox Vernon said.

"Just telling."

"I asked about Neil O'Neill," Fox Vernon said, letting it drop like a sack of flour falling ten stories.

Drover didn't say anything.

"He's got a lawyer trying to figure out the easiest way to divorce Mrs. O'Neill without paying a lot of alimony. He's got a girl in every port and two on the starboard side. The high life agrees with him. He bad-mouths Paul Givens as much as he bad-mouths his ex-wife. He is probably nasty to little children too."

"My kind of guy," Drover said. "Why doesn't he blow the whistle on St. Mary's?"

"Because he doesn't want to blow the whistle on himself."

"Would television care? I mean, would it affect his career?" Drover said.

"Come on, Drover. How many ex-jocks are on TV living down their college pasts when they did bad recruiting? Lots. TV doesn't care, the fans don't care, the colleges don't care unless they get caught at it and lose a season of TV revenues. The only ones who care are the old ladies on the board of governors."

"You've been in Vegas too long. You're cynical, Foxy. Get out in the world. Go to Indiana, watch basketball where it's still played with peach baskets."

"I was in Indiana once for something. A bee bit me and I was sick for days," Fox Vernon said.

"Nature lover," Drover said. "I'm keeping the room but I'm going down to Indiana tonight."

"Talk to anyone in particular?"

"A few people," Drover said. "I guess I just didn't believe that Dan Briggs killed himself but then I couldn't think of any other reason to explain his being dead. His bookie isn't going to kill him if he owes the bookie money. Break his legs maybe but not kill. So you run a spreadsheet on Briggs and it turns out possible he might be fixing points for someone. For something."

"It's called money."

"Everyone likes to think the ref done it. It's a sports cliché."

"College zebras don't make much. They do it for the love of the game," Fox Vernon said.

"Yeah," Drover said. "Don't we all?"

"You want to try out as an NCAA investigator, Drover? I thought your checkered past would preclude that."

"Someone asked me a favor. The more I get into it, the more curious I get. On my own peg. My own time. My own money, if you want it that way."

"Peace, kemo sabe. I want to know what's going on. I live in a world without windows. Make me see the light."

"I want to see it myself."

"Just think about this—that maybe you're wrong, maybe Briggs got remorse or whatever you call it and killed himself."

"It doesn't happen as often as you think."

Silence on the line.

"No." Fox Vernon took a sigh. "If it did, Vegas would be back to being a cowboy town."

"So straighten up your cynicism and pull up your socks," Drover said. "I'll see us through on this."

"But be careful."

"Yes, Mommy," Drover said. And they broke the connection between one reality and another.

ELEVEN

Sᴛ. Mᴀʀʏ's Bulldogs beat themselves. Polanski couldn't buy a basket and Albert Brown fouled out in the third quarter. Penn State wasn't that good; St. Mary's was that bad, and it showed, even on the car radio.

Drover listened to the results on the weak-signaled station out of Chicago and then gave it up. Static and snow were in the air. Indiana was a mess. Chicago was basking in temperatures in the twenties on a clear night but from the Indiana-Illinois line east, it was hell. The prevailing northwest winds were whipping down Lake Michigan and turning into snow in northern Indiana and southern Michigan. The toll road was closed and Drover took the back way down two-lane highways he remembered from his school days. He almost lost it twice and his hands were tight and numb from holding the steering wheel when he reached the outskirts of North Fork, Indiana.

Fionna was waiting for him at the Motel 6 south of downtown.

He hated North Fork and any thought of old home week. He

had never gone back to the school except to fly in and scout games and fly right out again. And he didn't look forward to trying to build up a conversation with Paul Givens.

Fionna was wearing jeans and a thick sweater. She looked smaller and even more vulnerable. Her ivory skin was whiter than it should have been.

She had secured him a room on the same floor at the other end of the hall and he dropped his single bag on the bed, turned on the TV to make sure it worked, and followed Fionna to her room.

She sat on the bed and he took the chair. The beds were made up and her single bag was open on the desk-cum-TV stand.

Her black hair was long and tied with a pink length of yarn. She didn't wear any makeup and she didn't need to, Drover thought. Her eyes were enough to make any room warm.

"Tough game," Drover said.

"I listened to the game," she said. "When I was at Paul's house trying to get through to Betsy."

"Did you get through?"

"She said Paul's been upset but that she told him that he couldn't stand success and that he should listen to Father O'Brien and finally, she said, Paul just stopped talking to her about his problem," Fionna said. She said it without holding back a trace of contempt. "The world is make-believe to people like Betsy."

"Maybe they're right," Drover said. "If Betsy can close her eyes and make the boogeyman disappear, more power to her."

"Do you think I should talk to Father O myself?" Fionna said.

"About what? Is Father O'Brien going to tell you the truth any more than he has already told Paul?"

"You don't like him. I forgot that. You didn't like him when you were here," she said.

"He's very likable and that's why I don't trust him. He's a greeter and a glad-hander. Maybe he's making Paul nervous."

"What should I do?"

"Neil is going to divorce you," Drover said. He wondered why he said it. He knew then but he couldn't admit it right away. He wanted to take Fionna Givens in his arms and kiss her until she smiled, and sleep with her all night long. There, that was admitting it, wasn't it?

She folded her arms and looked away, as though she might be ashamed of something. "I know that. I suppose I've just been waiting for it."

"You got a good lawyer?" Drover said.

"You ought to mind your own business," Fionna said. She wasn't looking at him but staring at the snowy night under the streetlamps outside her window.

"Dan Briggs reffed games at St. Mary's. Three games last year and St. Mary's beat the spread. A lot of Midwest money goes down on St. Mary's, football and basketball," Drover said. "Dan Briggs had money problems too. There are lots of temptations out there."

"You think Paul did something?" She was looking right at him now and her folded arms were defiant and her eyes were burning into him.

Drover got up from the chair and went to the window. He needed a moment of staring into space. Then he turned to Fionna sitting on the edge of the bed.

"Why don't I ask him? You called me, Fionna, not the other way around. So far I've talked to two cops, a bookmaker in a dive on the northwest side of Chicago, and a guy I trust in Las Vegas. You and Paul and Neil O'Neill were one cozy little family, weren't you?"

"What do you mean?"

"Paul worked for Neil. You were married to Neil. It never crossed your mind that maybe Neil cut corners as coach? Come on, Fionna, I knew from the minute you and I went to that coffeehouse that there was something else going on. I'm semistupid, like in telling you something you already know like Neil's getting a divorce from you, but I have a good heart."

She was angry and it showed. She stood up and looked him in the face. "You think I care about anything except Paul?"

"You care about Neil. Did anyway. You married him."

"You do a lot of silly things when you're young," Fionna said.

"And now we're not as young as we were," Drover said in a gentler voice.

"Neil cheated on me. You think I want to tell a man that? Or tell myself? Neil cheated on me every chance he got and everyone knew it and I thought I wasn't good enough or I wasn't doing the right thing or . . . shit, I was blaming myself because he couldn't keep it in his pants. And I loved him. That's the other part. He could crawl into my bed anytime and it was all right then, but you keep fooling yourself . . ."

She was crying through the anger. The tears were large and ran down her cheeks and she didn't make a move to wipe them away. He wanted to say something but there were too many words already. So he just hugged her, the way a friend hugs a friend. That's what he told himself he was doing.

She shuddered as she cried and buried her face in his chest.

When the crying was past, they got in his car and took a drive toward the lights of North Fork. It was nearly ten at night and the town was settled in for the night, drawing the fields of snow over itself like covers and sleeping without dreams. Only a few taverns were left open for the lonely hearts and insomniac travelers.

The place was called Farmer's Inn, and a few of the denizens had been overserved. There was a John Wayne Western on the television set, and the guy behind the bar was named Curly because he was completely bald.

They sat away from other people. Someone put a quarter in the jukebox and Waylon and Willie began telling the world sad stories over the drumbeats of their guitars.

"I suppose I wouldn't put anything past Neil," she said, staring at her glass of beer and wiping the cold sweat on it with her fingertips. "He did that favor for Paul. I just about forgave him everything because of that. He lobbied hard for Paul with Father O'Brien."

"Father O'Brien wanted someone else to succeed Neil when Neil went to television?"

"There're all kinds of rivalries in a place like St. Mary's. Four years ago, Father O'Brien brought in a new athletic director named Dave Zekman. He's a very high-powered type. He didn't move against Neil but he was busy with the football team. He shoved out the coach the way you'd run over a ground squirrel on the road and not think

about it. There was a change in the philosophy of the athletic department. It wasn't for the good. Even Neil said he felt nervous. That's
when we were still talking to each other."

"You like this guy a lot."

"I wasn't afraid of him. Neil wasn't afraid of him. Neil said if
Zekman tried to make a move on him, he'd hand him his balls in a
jar of Vaseline."

"Neil is certainly a colorful talker, no wonder he gets on so well
on the tube."

"Zekman wanted to do a total shake-up in the basketball program
when Neil said he was going to television. Top to bottom, even to
probably getting rid of old Red Matlock on the radio broadcasts."

Drover shook his head. "Say it isn't so, not old Red. Tsk, Tsk."

"Zekman doesn't have any loyalty—"

"But he got a TV deal with the football program that pays St.
Mary's twenty-eight mill over the next seven years. Father O would
say that buys a lot of chalk and erasers," Drover said.

"But it's all just so ruthless."

Drover looked at her. "Fionna, you say Betsy doesn't have a grasp
of reality. How about a coach's wife who actually believes in Santa
Claus and pure sport for the fun of it? Wouldn't that be you?"

"Neil was a good coach, he didn't carry the game home with
him," Fionna said. She bit at the words in anger. Maybe at him,
maybe at herself.

"Like Paul does. With you."

"That isn't fair."

"So Neil carried water for Paul with Father O and the good
reverend granted Paul's wish to succeed Neil as head coach of the
Bulldogs."

"Yes. Neil did it. Zekman made no secret that he didn't want
Paul."

"Why?"

"Because Paul isn't well known enough, because none of the shoe
companies wanted him to endorse their products, because of a lot of
things. Mainly, Zekman doesn't think that Paul can recruit for St.
Mary's."

"He's got a good team."

"Which he inherited from Neil. Neil did the recruiting. With Neil gone, Zekman thinks that a lot of kids won't want to go to St. Mary's with a no-name coach."

Drover nodded. He waved a finger and Curly came down the boards with two more beers. Willie was saying on the jukebox that he was a highwayman and across the dusty roads he did ride with a pistol by his side. John Wayne was posing on the TV in that peculiar, loose-limbed ballet dancer's way of his.

"Dave Zekman. Where did he come from? I mean, his name came up when they announced the TV deal for football but I wasn't overly interested then," Drover said.

"He developed the program at University of Santa Fe. Did the same things. Came in and shook up first the basketball program and then went after football."

"Santa Fe U, the nonlearner's school. That's right. Dave Zekman. I don't keep up with college ball like I should," Drover said. He tasted the beer. "My trouble is that I like sports where the greed is pure and unstrained, like pro football. I hate to get preached at while someone is picking my pocket."

"College sports is no different from anything else in life," Fionna said.

"Unfortunately," Drover said.

She bent her head down now, saying something that was going to be hard to say, reaching for the words.

"I'm thirty-six years old and that's not old and not young, it's just there," she said. "I didn't have children. Maybe if I had had children, everything would look different. I got married to a man who showed me I was the married one, not him. I even found out he cheated on me on our goddamned honeymoon. What does that say about me, let alone him?"

Drover knew it was self-pity. You beat yourself up to feel better. Well, self-pity was as honest as any other emotion, wasn't it?

He waited while Fionna lashed herself some more. "I was in love with him, everything about him, the way he looked and laughed and talked and . . . well, there it is. I was the one in love, not him. I don't have anything. I know he's probably scheming on how he's going to get out of giving me anything. What he doesn't know is I don't want anything. I don't want a damned thing. He said I could have the house when he was packing his bags. A hundred-and-fifty-thousand-dollar house with a forty-thousand-dollar mortgage. I sold the house in six months and he didn't squawk. Just flew in on closing day and signed the papers and turned around and went back to New York. He looked right through me, Jim."

"Divorces happen, Fionna."

"Not to me, Jimmy. I was beautiful and men were in love with me. I could pick and choose."

"They're still in love with you," Drover said.

She looked at him and gave him a sad smile. "I've got gray hairs."

"You're beautiful," Drover said.

The smile turned up a little, not quite so sad, but still with a note of pity in it. "That's nice."

"Do you remember someone named Tommy Gallagher?"

"I think so. I went out with him a couple of times. He was a veteran, I think he was kind of scary."

"He's still scary. He's a cop. He's doing me a favor for you. For the memory of you."

"What favor?"

"Running something down," Drover said. "See, there're all kinds of guys in love with you."

"And I picked the rat of the bunch."

Drover didn't say anything.

Kris Kristofferson was saying he was broke in Baton Rouge or something like that. It made perfect sense at eleven at night in a snowbound town in the middle of nowhere.

"Paul just wouldn't come back from something like that. The mean things someone said about him. He's just starting out. They'd get rid of him. Where would he go?"

"He's thirty-four, thirty-five? He's hardly in the position of some guy getting laid off at age fifty-seven."

"But he didn't do anything," she said.

"Neither did the guy who turned fifty-seven. People lose their turn in line. I know about that." Drover made a face at himself. Self-pity was all right for the other guy, not him. "Fionna. I have to talk to him. He won't want to talk to me but I have to talk to him. I've got to see where he's coming from. The problem is that I am not the sort of guy that a college coach under investigation wants to be seen talking to."

"Oh." She turned to him as suddenly as a thought. She took his hand. "Oh, Jimmy. I'm sorry. I think and think about my own problem, about Paul, and then I flare up at you and I forget what you're doing. For me."

It was nice to have his hand held. He let her keep doing it.

"Paul'll talk to you if I have to drag him," she said.

"Make it easier than that. Give him a ride to work tomorrow morning and make sure he goes with you. You run him up to Michigan City, there's a McDonald's on forty-twenty-one going into town. About eleven."

"Why all the way to Michigan City?"

"Because it's the last place on earth anyone would meet any-one about anything," Drover said. "No one there will know me or Paul or you. Check out the rearview mirror in case you're being fol-lowed."

"Followed? Why would I be followed?"

"The NCAA could have hired more than one investigator. Put together a paper trail. See who Paul meets with."

"I wouldn't know what to do if someone was following me."

"Don't do anything if you suspect it. Just drive on by. I don't think they're going to spend the time and manpower to follow you but it can happen. If it doesn't, meet me at the sign of the Big Mac. We'll have a McLean Deluxe and a diet something and chat. Then you can drive him home for his car and I'll drive back to Chicago," Drover said.

"What then?"

"I'll drop a dime on this guy Gallagher and we'll see what he got out of this," Drover said.

"You can't talk to anyone at the NCAA, you said they think you're a crook."

"If I have to, I can talk to anyone. Without making faces. Besides, you gave me a name and I have to run a little check on him. Dave Zekman."

*   *   *

It was time to go and they knew it. They rode back to the Motel 6 in silence, separated in thought, apart from each other on the broad bench seat. The snow was being plowed off the roads and all would be well in the morning.

Drover walked her to her door and waited while she opened it with her key. Then he said good-night and went to the other end of the hall.

He closed the door and undressed.

In the darkness, he lay naked in bed and thought about Fionna Givens and how they had all been younger once and how they had grown older and more disappointed with the way things turned out. He thought of the cop, Tommy Gallagher, and thought Gallagher was just as disappointed as anyone at the way things turned out but hid it with doll's china mask of false cynicism. He was as fragile as his mask.

It really didn't surprise him when she knocked at the door. He opened it and she slipped inside the room and into his arms.

She made love with a kind of false desperation that hurtled itself at his body. He said soft things to her and kissed her quiet until she could be held in his arms. He made love to her and it was as good as he had ever wanted it to be, yearning for her years ago at the threshold of his life, not realizing they would ever reach this moment. When they weren't young.

TWELVE

T HE DAY was bright, sunny and cold, and Drover was into his second Styrofoam cup of coffee when he saw Fionna pull her Toyota into the parking lot of the McDonald's. The shift was changing in the restaurant; the old-timers who fed themselves endless refills of free coffee in midmorning were making way for mothers and toddlers. The menu was changed over from instant breakfast to instant lunch. The ordered inevitability of it depressed Drover. So did the thought of what he would say to Paul Givens.

Paul was frowning and Fionna was frowning and it was not going to be a meeting of happy campers. They had probably shouted at each other for thirty-five miles.

Paul sat down across from Drover and gave him a look that could freeze a starting forward who has a string of bad shots. It was the iron under the soft, young features of his face; all the good coaches have that look.

But Drover decided he wasn't a basketball player and wasn't going to be afraid. "Hi, Paul."

"So what's your interest in this?"

"How you doin', Paul?"

"I asked Fi and she said you were doing her a favor. I can't speak for her but I don't need favors."

"Who set you up?" Drover said.

"I am not going to talk about an ongoing investigation with an ex-sportswriter who works for gamblers," Paul said. "I told you that, Fi. I don't have to talk to him."

Drover thought about a left-handed approach. The only trouble with lying is making sure you keep the exaggeration down. "I'm more interested in Dave Zekman than you, Paul. The word in Vegas is that there's a big shake-up coming in the program at St. Mary's. That's why Fox sent me out, check it out. Your team stank up Pennsylvania last night."

Fionna had gone to the counter to buy coffees. She put them down on the table now and sat next to her brother and looked at his profile. Paul was busy glaring at Drover, thinking of three or four hundred well-chosen words to offer him.

"The team was upset. We play better than that."

"That's what I figured. You were favored by four."

"I don't give a damn about gambling odds," Paul said. He looked sharply at Fionna. "I told you some things once in confidence, you never had the right to bring in someone . . . like Jimmy Drover."

Drover held up his hand and smiled. It was an odd thing to do. It caught Paul's attention and his silence.

"Fionna. Go out to your car and start it. This won't take long and I can guarantee Paul'll be out in a minute."

She looked at him.

"I'll call you," Drover said. "You staying over a night at the Motel Six?"

"Yes—"

"I'll call you later," Drover said.

She got up and looked at Paul. Paul started to rise. Drover held up his hand again. "Siddown, Paul."

"I got nothing to say to you."

"I got something to say to you, though."

Fionna walked away. She was wearing boots and jeans and she made everything about her seem designed to be sexy. When they had awakened in the bright morning, they had smiled at each other and that had made it all right. Sometimes people make love for all the wrong reasons and it shows in the morning. Sometimes they get lucky.

Paul said, "Everyone can get examined by the NCAA. It isn't that uncommon. Lou Holtz, for Christ's sake, got investigated."

"And we all know he's a saint," Drover said. "The point is, what are you, Paul?"

"Why does it interest you?"

"Fionna interests me. You're less than zero. She wants a favor, I offered her a favor. Who wants your hide on the barn door?"

"No one. Everyone. You know what it is, you were a sportswriter. You're recruiting down at the high school level, all over the country. You go to the shoe camps, watch the kids, try to figure who can help you. And then you got to convince them to come aboard. You know what it is. It's a little of this and that. Neil O'Neill gave me a good team, and I can go up to the first ranks this year with it. If they don't lose their heads. Or their hearts. Like they did last night."

"Any recruiting problems would have pointed at Neil O'Neill when he was coach, not you," Drover said. "So what's the other shoe?"

"I can't talk about it."

"Oh come on. It's point shaving. Maybe with the connivance of some zebras. That's why Fionna came to me. She thinks I know the bad guys." Drover picked up his paper cup of coffee. "I do, in fact."

"What bad guys?"

"Refs fix games. Players fix games. It happens. Some chiseler wants an edge, he buys a ref. Not that often but it happens. Same with players."

"St. Mary's is clean . . ."

"So tell me about Dave Zekman and why he doesn't like you."

Paul sighed. The restaurant was kitchen-bright with sun, and the kids ran around their patient mothers like terriers. "We have different ideas, different ways of putting the program into motion."

"I called a lot of people this morning," Drover said. "Zekman is a money A.D. That means he professionalizes athletic programs to

97

maximize profit for the college or university he works for. I want to use the big words because you've been around the academic setting long enough to think they're normal speech. He did it at Santa Fe, and he's going to do it at St. Mary's. Which is a shame in a way, because St. Mary's is a better school than that, but someone decided it needed to squeeze the golden goose a little harder."

"Look. I just want to coach basketball, I don't interfere with Zekman or anyone. Father O'Brien picked me for coach—"

"Is Father O still behind you a thousand percent?"

It was a good question. Drover saw the flash of pain cross the iron eyes. Good. That would lead to something.

"Yes," Paul said. It had taken him too long.

"Father O brought in Zekman."

"Maximize the earning potential on the football side. You got to admit he engineered a helluva television deal." Was that resentment?

"And what about basketball? You and Neil had a lock on the program for what? Ten years. Neil was head coach and you were first assistant and you guys had a life. Then Neil decides to go network and he does you the big favor of getting you the job when the athletic director wasn't crazy about you. Why'd he do that, Paul?"

"We were co-workers. We were friends."

"You still friends?"

Again, pain across the iron. Paul was taking too long. Drover felt a pang of sympathy. Paul made the sign of the cross when he shot free throws, he preached the brotherhood of men, decency in sports, and probably prayed every night. Drover could see how hard it was for him to lie. He was thinking better of Paul despite himself.

"Neil said something that wasn't so," Paul said.

"What did he say?"

"He told Cary Lucas—yes, you know about Cary Lucas—he told Cary Lucas that I recruited Albert Brown on my own. That just wasn't so. I scouted him at the Nike camp in Indianapolis when he was in his junior year and I made charts on him and recommended him to Neil. I even went down to North Carolina twice to talk to him, his mother, talk to the nuns at his school, but it was Neil who was the recruiter, and now he just says he took credit for it. At least, that's the way I got it. Neil never said he went to North Carolina. Never. I've tried to reach him but he's been out of town. I know that Neil must have been misunderstood or something—"

"Why would he say that?"

Silence. Muzak was doing a ditty based on Mrs. Robinson and a woman at the counter was demanding a McLean Deluxe without salt. It was like asking for a Big Mac without calories.

"I don't know. I don't understand any of this. Why it blew up before the season stated. This season of all seasons, we've got a first-class team. Damnit."

Paul sat there making a fist, hitting the table softly with his hand. "You can go your life in coaching and not have a chance at the Four. You know the jealousies we have. Indiana, Illinois, Notre Dame, DePaul, Iowa, Ohio State, I mean, just in the Midwest, we're re-cruiting against each other like mad and there're rules inside of rules about what we can do and what we can't and when you get a good player, you stir up the other coaches. Sometimes they make accusations. It's tough."

"Paul, why would Neil lie about you?"

"Because . . . I don't know. Is he mad at me because of what happened between him and Fionna? I never interfered except I told Fionna she should stand by her husband—"

"Good sound Catholic advice."

"I'm not ashamed of being a Catholic," Paul said. "You're a Catholic."

He said it evenly, not even asking for a fight, just stating a conviction. "It didn't work out and when a marriage goes, there're a lot of reasons. Maybe blame on more than one side. Maybe because they didn't have children after all those years."

Drover wanted to change the subject. "The referee who killed himself. Dan Briggs. He was betting on games with a bookie in Chicago. I got a cop looking into it. Maybe the rest of this is smoke and maybe this is about something else. Maybe a zebra was making bad calls for a gambler to beat the spread in games he reffed and maybe someone is covering it up with this stuff about St. Mary's kids' point shaving.

"They're good kids. I'm with them twelve months a year. I go to their homes. I know their families. They're good kids," Paul said.

"I'm not your enemy, Paul," Drover said. It was meant as sympathy, but Drover saw it came out wrong.

The iron came back in Paul's eyes. It was stubborn and it was as cold as an iron fence on a winter day.

"Fine, I've got enough as it is," Paul said. "But that doesn't make you my friend. Don't do me favors. Don't use my name and don't come around me or my team. Okay? I listened to you because of Fionna. And now I'm going back home and report this to the NCAA."

"Don't do yourself harm," Drover said.

"Sure. Don't report an illegal contact with a gambler. You must think I'm nuts, both of you, Fionna and you. I don't know what this is, but I'm going to tell them everything we just talked about," Paul said.

Drover shrugged. He got up and looked down at Paul. He shook his head. "You're too good to be true," he said. Funny. He said it wistfully.

"How would you know?" Paul said. "Just stay away from me, from Fionna, from the team. You do your dirty work for yourself. Don't come back for any reunions, okay?"

"Okay," Drover said. He said it light. When you keep it light, the contempt in the other's voice doesn't hurt as much. "Your funeral, Paul. And I'll skip the wake."

THIRTEEN

Drover DROPPED off the rental car at the Avis garage on Clark Street and decided to walk across the Loop toward his hotel. The day was almost balmy—near forty and full of sun—and the gutters were wet with melting snow. He had thought about it all the way back from Indiana and decided it was the best thing. Let Paul bring him into the picture and wait for the NCAA to drop a dime on him. It made him feel a bit naked but that had happened before.

A block from the Drake at the head of Michigan Avenue, he saw the car. Some cars never change, even when the models do. This was a Cadillac with blacked-out grill, smoked windows, and the peculiar dove-gray paint job that General Motors does so well.

The rear door on the sidewalk side opened and Drover paused. The big car was parked in a tow-away zone and there was a traffic cop on the corner and Drover just knew the car had permission to sit there until Judgment Day without getting a ticket or a tow.

"Get in, Drover," Vin said. He was behind door number two,

in the back. Another muscle was driving. Vin used words as carefully as a miser spending dimes. He had started life with just so many dimes and he was going to make them last.

"I got places to go and people to see," Drover said.

"Nothing is as important as this," Vin said. More dimes off the roll of life. It must have been important.

Drover slid into the backseat and dropped his overnight bag on the cushions. The car was as quiet as a grave, a cliché that Drover didn't want to really think about.

Vin wore a turtleneck sweater over his bulk and a down jacket. He stared straight ahead. "Go on," he told the driver. The driver was new to the entourage, Drover saw.

The car rolled along East Lake Shore Drive and doubled back to the lower level of Wacker. They were going west, which was a good sign. Tony Rolls lived west. You didn't do bad business where you slept. At least Drover hoped so.

Tony Rolls was a retired mobster who manuevered through life now in a wheelchair. There had been a time when his horse-choker hands could have killed a horse (some say they did once) and he puffed up his muscle by carrying rolls of quarters in each mitt. Tony Rolls, now retired from crime activity in the Outfit, was living out his pension years in a pile of stone in River Forest, west of the city.

Drover had not come from such a grand neighborhood, but then neither had Tony Rolls in the beginning. Drover's upbringing was on a west side block of the city where cops and firemen, crooks and politicians, sportswriters and businessmen, came from. He was a victim of his colorful past. He knew the right people and too many of the wrong. Funny how they all turned out, different tastes from the same melting pot. He had known Captain Carmody as well as Tony Rolls, and if they admitted it to anyone, Carmody and Rolls knew each other too. The trouble was, Drover didn't want to know Tony Rolls all that well.

"How's Tony?" Drover said to Vin.

Vin grunted.

"You're a fascinating conversationalist."

"Fuck you," Vin said.

"I bet you say that to all the boys."

Vin didn't say anything. Traffic was light on the Eisenhower Expressway and the line was long at the Harlem exit.

Tony Rolls had a driveway with a gate across it. There was an iron deer on the wide lawn.

Drover got out and reached for his bag.

"Leave it," Vin said. Another good sign. He wasn't going to be asked to stay long.

Tony Rolls had a voice like an El train and muscles that strained beneath the self-indulgent layers of pasta-fed fat. His wheelchair was as massive as the man and, in a way, as dignified. The big house was dark without seeming gloomy. A cardinal in the Curia would have found it domestic.

Drover sat down in the leather wing chair across from the big man and rested his elbows on knees.

Tony Rolls just stared at him for a long moment. That was not a good sign. There were guys who swore that Tony Rolls got more out of a stare than Jack Benny ever did, and it wasn't laughs. His eyes were green olives that gave away nothing. The silence was broken by Tony's wheezy sigh.

"What are you doin' in Chicago?" Tony Rolls said.

"Visiting."

"You got no one to visit."

"I saw the captain."

"That asshole," Tony Rolls said. "How is he?"

"He sends his regards to you."

"Is that right?"

"No, it's a lie."

"That's more like it."

Silence.

"You wanna glass of wine?"

"It makes me sleepy in the middle of the day."

"All right. Vin. Gimme a glass of the new Chianti, I wanna try it."

Drover waited. The glass was fetched. Tony Rolls poured, tasted, let the bouquet of it settle on his taste buds. It was a nice show.

"Good stuff," Tony Rolls said. "Whyn't you try it? Get him a glass, Vin."

Drover thought one refusal was about all that Tony Rolls would accept. He took the wine and drank.

"Now, Vin, you and Vito go away, leave us to talk."

Vin and Vito, the new man, got up together and left the room.

"Well, whaddaya say, kid?"

"What do you want me to say?"

"Tell me about you and the cops. You got some cop coming down on some people I know," Tony Rolls said. "I'm not condemning it, you got a right, it's a free country, but I want to understand it."

"What do you not understand?"

"What's your interest in Dan Briggs?"

"He's dead, for one thing. He was a ref for another thing. He was accused of creative refereeing by someone and it got to the NCAA. And then he killed himself."

"That makes him interesting to you?"

"Look, Tony. Fox Vernon pays me money to sniff into things like that. He doesn't want to get caught with his lines down."

"Fox Vernon is a very smart oddsmaker. He don't get caught too often," Tony Rolls said.

"I'll pass on the compliment."

"But that don't tell me about what you wanna come down on a bookie named Myers for. What is this about, kid?"

"Somebody comes down on . . . what's it about with you? I don't know what you're talking about."

"I just like to understand things," Tony said.

"So do I."

"Then you start. Tell me about this cop friend of yours. This Mick named Tommy Gallagher. He suddenly shows up and he's not very nice, he gives Leo Myers a hard time. A hard time, you know. Irish asshole. So what's this got to do with you?"

"What's Leo to you, Tony?"

"I never met the man. I know someone who was . . . connected with this Leo Myers, perhaps a business associate."

"The guy he pays the street tax to," Drover said.

"There you go, all you fucking guys watch *The F.B.I.* on TV and you suddenly know everything about our thing. We're talking about one thing and you start telling me about some bullshit about street tax."

"All right, it's bullshit."

"All right. You like the wine?"

"I told you, it makes me sleepy. Nice wine."

"Very nice wine," Tony Rolls said.

"What do you know about a ref fixing games? Was he fixing them for your . . . friends?"

Tony Rolls smiled at that. "Good, kid. I like it when you come right out and take a shot at it. That's the way to do things. All right, I'll tell you the truth. Until today, I don't even know you're in town. Now I know. You send that Mick cop after a book, what's that to me? Or anyone. But then it gets more complicated and the cop, this Gallagher, he makes it sound like someone whacked this guy, this Dan Briggs."

He did, eh? Drover chewed that one over. Gallagher had come on stronger than Drover could have hoped for.

"Did someone whack him?"

"Who knows? People die. Ain't the cops supposed to know that?"

"They say it was suicide."

"Then they should know."

"But what do you say, Tony?"

"I don't say nothing, kid. We didn't even have this conversation, did we?"

"I keep running into people who talk to me but don't want to admit it. It makes me feel like I should check out my antiperspirant."

"Like who?"

"That would be telling," Drover said.

Tony Rolls sighed and put down his glass on the side table. "Drover, you think there was point shaving, you should go to the FBI, you should not be involving yourself in lowlifes. You ain't got the weight for it, capeesh? I'm telling you because I like you. Guys like this Gallagher, dime-a-dozen cops, and guys like this book and maybe some of his associates. You know that's their business and I don't interfere with them, I'm retired."

"Don't they need permission to put out a hit on someone?"

"The fuck you doing, watching *Godfather* reruns? The fuck you think this thing works? This is a side deal, if it's anything. I don't know about no fix, I don't wanna know."

Drover put down his glass too. He leaned forward. "Tony, you're so full of shit your eyes are turning brown. If there's a college fix, Tony Rolls and all of Tony's uncles and nephews in Vegas want to know about it. Unless they put it together in the first place."

"Young guys, they sometimes get an idea to do something, they don't follow through with their thinking, thinking about who this might hurt. They're kids," Tony Rolls said. "You get me? It ain't in anyone's interest that I can see to fix games because we make the money on the sport of the thing, on the odds, not on fixing games."

"You make money every which way you can."

Tony turned over his hands to show his honesty. They did not have rolls of quarters in the palms.

"Some people say that."

"You hear about St. Mary's?"

"I heard the minute the N C Double A put out an investigation on it."

"They didn't hear in Vegas." Drover was thinking of Fox Vernon.

"Not everyone in Vegas got as big a set of ears as I do," Tony Rolls said. The smile showed yellow, strong teeth.

"What's the story?"

"Hey, I don't know the whole thing. Was some guys shaving? That's what they want to know. Maybe kids on the team. Maybe there was kink going on with the coach. Present and past. You see him on TV?"

"Yeah," Drover said, thinking of Neil and thinking what it would be like to talk to him face-to-face knowing he had made love to his wife.

"Nice show. Knows his stuff. I watch it." Silence. "Maybe he got out of St. Mary's College at the right time, before it hit the fan."

"I've thought of that," Drover said.

"Good. But what I want to know is, kid, and I want you to tell me, is why are you working so hard on this?"

"The good of the game."

"Bullshit."

106

"All right, Fox Vernon already doesn't know half of what you told me, about the investigation."

"If he don't know, why are you here?"

"I was here to see some games. The Bulls. Went to DePaul the other night. Saw St. Mary's play."

"All right." Held up his hand. "You want to tell me that stuff, all right. I know you're doing this for some reason but I'm not gonna knock it out of you. Just this, kid, and I mean it. There are dangerous people out there sometimes. It ain't like it was me or anyone doing something. Sometimes, they're just crazy, they gotta make their bones, prove themselves. You see what I mean? You might wanna be very careful is what I'm saying. I knew you when you were this high, I like to keep knowing you a while longer."

And Drover, for the first time since Fionna called to him on the street that night, saw how bad it really might be.

FOURTEEN

"WHAT DO YOU think, Dave?" Father O'Brien said. They had been sitting in the president's office for two full silent minutes. Paul Givens had left for his regular postgame team meeting. He had told them everything.

"What do you think?"

"He told the truth," the priest said.

"Absolutely what I was thinking."

"He did the right thing coming to us. Telling us right away."

"Absolutely what I was thinking," Dave Zekman said. He had a habit of making a church steeple with his fingers. His face was drawn because he believed in semistarvation as a way to good health. His sleek head of straight-back hair was shiny under the strong ceiling lights in the room.

Father O'Brien settled farther into the swivel chair behind his massive rosewood desk. He didn't like this at all, none of it.

"What do we do?" the priest said.

"We notify Cary Lucas right away. The NCAA has to be informed. I think this is a bad turn for us. For St. Mary's."

"You mean they're going to take it the wrong way."

"Definitely. I know the NCAA."

"But Paul is completely innocent of—"

"Neil O'Neill said he did not recruit Albert Brown, just put Paul on the case because Paul was close to the boy. Whatever violations they are finding out in North Carolina, it's going to reflect on Paul. And now a known gambler—"

"I don't know that Drover is a gambler—"

"A man once indicted by a federal grand jury for his connection with professional gamblers, with the Mafia, for the love of God," Dave Zekman said. He broke up the church steeple and grasped the arms of the leather wing chair. "He comes out here, to this school, and he brings up all this about the referee who killed himself and he acts like he is doing Paul a favor. A favor. A favor like that, you don't need more than one a decade."

"Paul is a decent man," Father O'Brien said.

"I believe he is," Dave Zekman said. "I also think until this thing is cleared up, he should step aside. I mean, the future of the season is at stake."

"They were lousy last night, just lousy," Father O'Brien said. "Maybe they're not as good as we hoped they would be."

"Oh, they're good, they're just spooked by the NCAA investigation. And it isn't going to get better until the thing is settled. The NCAA might go at this for a year or more and then what does that do to our program, to our recruiting program? Or the reputation of the school itself?"

"What you want is for Paul to resign."

"No. Not resign. Not at all. It's an option but it's Paul's decision, he has a contract going one more season. I'm just saying that we have to see where this Cary Lucas is going to take this case."

"Why would Drover want to hurt St. Mary's? He was a student here," Father O'Brien said. "I believe he was in one of my theology classes."

"People change. I think we have to be open and honest with the NCAA, we don't want to hurt our full program. We have a football team to think about too. They start worrying at some detail and they want to open the whole can of worms."

Father O'Brien let his eyes settle hard on his athletic director. He paused a long moment. "Is there a can of worms, Dave? I mean, in the football program?"

"Not at all. The point is, everyone is guilty of something. What you would call original sin, I guess. Everyone, no matter how hard they try, can't live up to the Ten Commandments. And the NCAA rule book is a lot longer."

The bells in the steeple of St. Mary's rang the Angelus. It was the middle of the day, and the Angelus call to prayer rang three times a day. As he always did when he heard the bells, Father O'Brien blessed himself. The act was without self-consciousness.

Dave Zekman waited.

"What do you suggest, Dave?"

"I call Cary Lucas, lay it out for him, seek his advice. He can't say we haven't been cooperative."

"No, he can't."

"I'll talk to Paul later, after I talk to Cary Lucas, see if we're all in on the same loop."

"And if we're not?"

"Paul will do the right thing. Right for him, right for the team, right for St. Mary's," Dave said.

"You didn't want him as head coach when Neil left. Did you know something then, something you didn't want to say at the time?"

Dave made a face that said he was thinking hard. "Not what you're implying. I thought Paul was a weak figure as head coach. This has nothing to do with his abilities, it has to do with the pressure of being a head basketball coach at a school with the . . . national mystique of St. Mary's. I was honest with you about that. St. Mary's can be a powerhouse in the game, not this year alone but for a lot of years. Neil O'Neill was a great figure, he gave good press conferences, he wrote op-ed pieces for the papers, he did TV talk shows. But what it came down to was that he never won the national championships. He was good for St. Mary's in his era but being a second-rate Neil O'Neill is not good for St. Mary's in the nineties." Dave Zekman was a decades quoter. Before he would have talked of a "team for the eighties," but times had changed, and talking about "the nineties" put him in the leading edge of the sound-bite school of philosophizing. "We need a strong leader. Not for this season but next season and the season after. Basketball is getting to be a very big business and we're not getting our fair share of it. We can. I think NCAA wants us to get a bigger share because it helps stir the pot when they negotiate with television. It benefits everyone to have a strong St. Mary's."

Except Paul Givens, Father O'Brien thought.

FIFTEEN

"WHO IS THIS guy?"

"Leo Myers says he don't know."

"Is that right? Is that what we go with, we don't know? I don't wanna hear 'don't know.' "

"Well, he was a newspaperman in Chicago once—"

"Fuckin' whores."

"Yeah well. He was indicted once in Los Angeles for some bullshit, federal bullshit, but they dropped the indictment. He ain't inside, if that's what you're asking, Steve."

"That ain't what I'm asking, I know that already. I wanna know what he's goin' around lookin' into our business about?"

Steve was riding around. He was tooling the big Buick Park Avenue like a scooter. He got maybe six, seven speeding tickets a year or illegal turn stuff, junk he turned over to his lawyer. He was thirty-six years old and never spent a night in jail unless you count the time he was picked up for smacking that cop around. Traffic cop gave him

113

a hard time about going through a red light. A broad, looked comical with that belt full of cuffs and Mace and a piece, he just had to smack her. That was as close as he had come to doing real time. Couple of years ago anyway.

Steve March could have had someone drive him, but that was for the old guys, the mustaches. Steve March said he relaxed when he was driving around, talking things out with someone like little Bugs here beside him in the front seat.

Bugs would rather have been in jail at the moment.

They were cruising up the Kennedy Expressway for no reason, going seventy or so through the northwest side of the city, heading for the airport, though that wasn't a destination.

"Who's Tommy Gallagher?"

"Cop out of central planning. Was a homicide dick."

"He's got time on his hands, fucking around with a book like Leo, what's he want? A shakedown? Mick bastards never work a day in their lives, just shaking down people for their change," Steve March said. His eyes were bulletproof, his whole manner carried an armor coating. When most people looked at him, they looked for ways to be nice to him.

"I should pick up this Drover," Steve March said. "Except I gotta know who his Chinaman is. He knows Tony Rolls, I heard enough about that. I give a fuck about Tony Rolls, crippled asshole. This Drover is what? English? Irish? All the same, potato eaters."

"He works for a book in Vegas name of Fox Vernon. He scouts out games, sniffs around at them to see what's what."

"So what's he sniffing about Dan Briggs for? Dan Briggs killed himself."

Bugs stared straight ahead. The big Buick was even passing cabs, they were going that fast. Steve would hit the horn, hit the brakes, swerve into another open lane, do the same thing. Bugs had a bad stomach.

"Cops know it, I know it. Then a cop comes up and puts the screws on Leo."

"Leo was like a sheet, he was that white."

"Fuck Leo. He don't say nothing."

"Leo wouldn't say nothing if they pulled his fingernails out."

"Because I could have his fingernails pulled out with pliers and make it last longer," Steve March said. You looked at him and heard him, you wouldn't think he was married with two kids in nice Catholic schools in Elmwood Park.

"He wouldn't do that."

Steve March pulled off at Lawrence and headed west for no reason, just to drive. He dropped the speed to forty on the street. He was a big and strong man but with a small man's restless energy. He didn't smoke or drink or do drugs. He was impatient with the deal life was laying out for him. He wasn't getting any younger.

Bugs was Bugs Rio, with watery eyes and the manner of a mortician, which is what his father had been. He collected the street tax from the bookies for Steve March. Steve really had it made, but he didn't see it that way. It went with being young.

"Whaddaya want me to do, Steve?"

Steve looked at him. The night was tawdry under the sodium-vapor lamps, casting orange shadows on dirty snowbanks. Nobody was walking unless they had to.

"Find out his clout, this Drover. Find out what he and this guy Tommy Gallagher are cooking. If they want a shakedown, we might have to deal with them. If it's something else, we might have to do something else."

"I'm working on it since today," Bugs said.

"Work harder."

Steve pulled up to the light at Lincoln Avenue and looked at Bugs. "Go on, Bugsie."

It was the end of the interview. Where the hell were they? Steve was always dumping him like this, it irritated Bugs along with a lot of other things about working for Steve. If you had asked Bugs—put it this way, if you had pulled out his fingernails with pliers to make sure he was telling you the truth—he would have told you Steve had a serious psychological problem.

He slammed the door behind him as the car darted through the green.

SIXTEEN

DROVER WAS surprised that Black Kelly was still in Maguire's, seemingly in the same spot at the back of the saloon, talking to the same off-duty firemen. He had threatened to go back to the sun and fun of the pier in Santa Cruz. Maybe old home week was sinking its hooks into him after all.

The firemen were red-faced and jolly. They were exchanging recipes. It was something firemen did. They were all chefs under the skin, no less than Kelly.

Drover joined them, nodded at the introductions, and bought a round.

"I was talking here to Noonan, he's got a great way to poach salmon fillets," Kelly said in his whiskey voice. His blue eyes were bright. Talking about food did that for them.

"Firehouse recipe," one of the firemen said. "You get a good fillet and you rub it down with a little lemon and put it in aluminum foil, see?"

Kelly couldn't stand not talking. "You put a little sauce in the foil or just some water, just to get it steaming and you wrap it up. Now, see, salmon is delicate and poaching is tricky. You don't want to overcook, burn it or make it tough. You see that?"

"You run a saloon on the pier in Santa Cruz and every place on it has fish and you only serve red meat dishes," Drover said. "I didn't suspect you were a fish gourmet too."

"There're lots of things you don't know. I can make a salmon mousse that would make a grown Frenchman cry." Kelly looked at his empty glass. "V.O. and soda," he said to the girl behind the bar. "A child's portion."

The other firemen were drinking beer, and Drover stuck with that. Tommy Gallagher had been out of pocket all day after Drover got back from his interview with Tony Rolls. He didn't know what he wanted to tell the cop in any case. He just knew that he felt better that Black Kelly had not abandoned him in Chicago. Tony Rolls had scared him right through.

"So you take the salmon," the fireman named Noonan began again.

"Lemme tell him, Noonan. You put the salmon in the top rack of your automatic dishwasher. And you put it through the cycle. Not the dry cycle, the wash cycle."

"I beg your pardon?" Drover said.

"See, an automatic dishwasher has the right temperature. Steam. You ever open a dishwasher in midcycle? It's all hot steam. That's perfect for poaching. And the salmon is protected from burning because it's on an open rack."

Drover shook his head. "You're driving me crazy again."

"It sounds crazy but it works," Noonan the fireman said. "You can feed a firehouse full doing it that way."

"I never used a dishwasher. Was this on Julia Child's show?"

"It could be," Black Kelly said. "She used a blowtorch once to make crepes, I saw it myself."

"Technology in the workplace," Drover said. "I got to make a call." He would normally not have chosen a public phone in a noisy place but he didn't want to be too far away from Kelly and the burly firemen or the warm lights of the bar. Maybe he was thinking it was a hard, cruel, and very cold city out there. Tony Rolls had painted it that way for him.

Fox Vernon in Las Vegas picked it up on the third ring.

"What is it?"

"The guy with NCAA is Cary Lucas. I told you that. I talked to Paul Givens. He's probably told everyone already that I talked to him. I swear he's a Boy Scout but someone has it in for him. Where's Neil O'Neill?"

"Ah, let me see." Pause. "He's doing the UCLA game tomorrow night, so I suppose he's in La-La. They usually stay at the Century Plaza."

"I'm going to surprise him," Drover said.

"I don't want to take St. Mary's bets after last night," Fox Vernon said. "They were terrible."

"Jitters is what Paul Givens said before he told me to mind my own business."

"What about my business?"

"Something deep is going on here. I got visited by a friend. Or an acquaintance at least who told me to back off a certain bookie who had certain dealings with the late Dan Briggs."

This wasn't a pause; this was a full-blown silence.

"So games were fixed."

"It's not right there, Foxy. It's on the edge of things, like footlights. I don't now how it all connects up, if it does. Paul Givens is in serious trouble and maybe this kid, this Albert Brown. I've got to see about that. Recruiting violations and it might have started with Neil O'Neill. Paul swears Neil recruited the kid and Neil told the NCAA that Paul handled the contract. So who's lying?"

"Who do you think?"

"I believe Paul. I'll bet he still knows the Scouting oath by heart," Drover said.

"Babies can drown in the waters where the sharks swim," Fox Vernon said.

Drover said, "What a way with words. No wonder you need a ghostwriter."

"I'm gonna talk this around," Fox Vernon said. "I don't want to be a chump about it."

"Talk it around but put in a good word for Paul Givens."

"Is this because of your keen, analytical reporting methods or because you have a crush on an old girlfriend?"

"Foxy, you shock me," Drover said.

They broke the connection.

SEVENTEEN

BLACK KELLY decided to wait in the bar with his buddies for the cows to come home. Drover was dead tired. Drover took a cab back to the Drake Hotel, thinking of poached salmon in the dishwasher and the fact that he couldn't reach anyone else on the phone—Fionna had checked out of her motel and Tommy Gallagher was not returning calls.

It was a clear midnight and the wind was coming off the lake, very cold and damp. The temperature had dropped into the twenties, and still there were people walking on the paths above the Oak Street beach, staring out at the night, thinking midnight thoughts. He paid the cab and went into the back entrance of the hotel on East Lake Shore Drive.

His room was crowded and the television set was on.

Tommy Gallagher was tieless, sitting in one of the easy chairs by the window, drinking a see-through. There was an ice bucket on the table and a white-clothed tray with sandwich remains on it. The other man was still in a suit, complete with tie, and had the familiar pallor of a dedicated man who knows no time schedule. His face was rock-hard, just like Tommy's.

Drover dropped his keys on the bed and waited. They were watching David Letterman do smart-ass things. Then Tommy reached for the remote and muted the sound.

"We were waiting for you," Tommy Gallagher said.

"I hope you made yourself at home."

"I didn't order pâté like I wanted, just club sandwiches," Tommy Gallagher said.

"And you, sir? Was the hospitality up to snuff?"

"My name is Peterson," the pallid man said. He was reaching for an ID wallet in his jacket on the back of the chair. Drover held up his hand.

"No need, I'll take your word for it," Drover said. He sat down on the edge of the bed and took off his shoes. His feet hurt. He rubbed a stockinged foot and looked at the two of them.

"Who you been seeing?" Peterson said.

"Who are you to ask?"

"I was gonna show you."

"All right. I don't need bullshit cards. I can get all the IDs I want."

"It's against federal law to pose as a federal officer," Peterson said.

"So you're a G," Drover said. "What are you getting me into, Gallagher?"

Gallagher smirked a little smile. It might have been embarrassment. "It's what I got into. I had a talk with that bookie. The name you gave me."

"Did I give you a name?"

"Fuck it, Drover, don't get cute, it's midnight, time to stop playing."

"What are we playing?"

"What's your interest in Dan Briggs?"

"I heard he killed himself because the NCAA was asking him questions about fixing college games," Drover said. "I didn't believe it."

"Why didn't you believe it?"

"I'm not as simpleminded as the cops," Drover said.

Gallagher did a full blush at that. "You are an asshole, you know that?"

"We assholes are never sure until we're certified by an asshole inspector. That's you," Drover said. He was very calm because this was his room and the TV was on and because it wasn't Tony Rolls warning about bad things that go bump in the night.

Peterson said, "You work for an oddsmaker in Las Vegas named Fox Vernon. You come to Chicago to ostensibly scout the strengths of various teams for the benefit of the oddsmaker. You involve yourself in an ongoing NCAA investigation that we were unaware of and you lead yourself to a bookmaker named Leo Myers. You involve Lieutenant Gallagher here in your investigation on behalf of a bookmaker. You both could be in trouble."

"Why is that?"

"Because . . ." Peterson was at a loss for words. It was so obvious. Then he tightened his face and made a small smile. It was halfway between Federal Agent Look Number One (we gotcha) and Number Three (we're all in this together).

"Because, let me finish, the FBI is involved, right? So you want to put the screws on Gallagher to lay off this bookie and to tell what he knows and you bring Gallagher along to my room and eat my food and drink my booze and watch my TV set to scare me. I ain't scared. I can be scared but this is ridiculous," Drover said. It was a long speech and he thought his hand was trembling. Anger or fright? What was behind Door Number Two anyway, besides Vin?

"Lieutenant Gallagher is cooperating," Peterson said. "I want you to cooperate."

Gallagher was watching Drover hard and Drover couldn't get any signal out of the stare. It was the flat station house stare, interested but uninterested at the same time, the one cops use when they're watching bugs get squashed.

"All right. I'll cooperate. What do you want me to say?"

"Why did you go to see Tony Rolls in River Forest this afternoon?"

"He wanted me to try a new wine. A Chianti. It was fine and I told him so."

"You think this is a joke?"

123

"You want a joke, I can tell you a new way to poach salmon fillets," Drover said.

"What if you were impeding a federal investigation?"

"What if you were charged with breaking and entering into my room?" Drover said. What was this about? He was playing it cool but cool only went so far. Cops and the G were the best at it, always had been.

"I don't suppose you've thought this out, Drover. This comes as a surprise to you, I can understand that." Peterson was slipping into Federal Agent Look Number Three. The smile was bigger. "I want to know what Tony Rolls had to say to you, and it will never leave this room."

"Sure," Drover said.

"Are you involved in illicit gambling activities?"

"I don't gamble. Come on, Gallagher, feel free to jump in at any time. You gonna let him beat us up?"

"Kemo sabe, he is only beating you up at the moment," Gallagher said.

"All right. Let's hang separately. I told Gallagher I didn't think that Dan Briggs killed himself because it wasn't logical. What's an NCAA investigation? What were they going to do to him?"

"Fixing games is against the law. State laws," Peterson said.

"Then what's the FBI in this?"

"There are interstate considerations."

"You guys are driving me crazy. You shouldn't watch so much television," Drover said. He got up just to do something. He went to the ice bucket and filled a glass with cubes and poured in a little vodka. Absolut. "You got this from room service? It probably costs forty bucks a bottle."

"Sixty, but who's counting," Gallagher said.

"Is this a legitimate expense, Peterson? Can I write it off?"

"You had trouble with our people before. You're a known associate of Outfit people," Peterson said.

Drover was still trying to think through it. He tasted the vodka and decided he couldn't taste it properly and put the glass down on the television set. David Letterman was smirking mutely.

"You think Dan Briggs was killed, right?" Drover finally said. He was staring at Peterson.

"Murder is not a federal offense."

"But you think he was killed. Both of you do."

"It's possible."

Drover made a face. He saw it now and saw the game the two of them were playing. He smiled at Gallagher. "How many times you talk to Leo?"

Gallagher looked at Peterson. "What's this guy? A cop all of a sudden?"

Drover waited a moment. "Okay. You talked to him twice."

"I did, huh?"

"First time you talked to him. Second time you came back at him with a hammer and tongs and practically certified that Dan Briggs had not killed himself. That he was whacked."

"I did, huh?"

"Sure. Because between the first time and the second time, you changed your mind. When you talked to me, you weren't sure about what I was saying. You probed around, very careful, like a cop that doesn't want to get mud on his spit shine. But you gave it to him hard the second time. That's called a cop with confidence." Drover looked at Peterson. "You gave him confidence, didn't you?"

Peterson went back to Look Number One. "Why don't you get on an airplane and go back to whatever scum you come from?"

"More like it." Drover smiled. "You guys are investigating something and it involves Leo Myers, right? And whoever Leo Myers deals with."

The silence was much longer. Someone in the room was deciding something.

"Put him under arrest," Peterson said to Gallagher.

Gallagher stared at the federal agent, and his mouth gaped.

"I want you to lock him up," Peterson said. "Withholding information or disorderly conduct or assaulting an officer. Yeah, he assaulted you."

"He assaulted me, he'd be eating through a straw," Gallagher said.

Drover laughed and turned his back and started for the bathroom.

"Put him away," Peterson said.

"I got nothing—"

"I'll give you something, Lieutenant," Peterson said. "You fucked this up already—"

Drover closed the bathroom door. And locked it. He picked up the phone by the toilet and punched in a number.

The door handle rattled.

"Come out of there," Peterson said.

"I'm taking a pee."

The connection at the other end was full of jolly, boozy noise. He said a name. A moment passed while they called out, "Black Kelly, Black Kelly!" around Maguire's bar.

"Captain Kelly," the voice said.

"You're not a captain anymore, Black," Drover said. "A cop named Tommy Gallagher is going to book me at First District in a few minutes. I want a lawyer. You call Fox Vernon in Vegas and get someone from Chicago."

"What did you do, kid?" Black Kelly said in a sudden sober voice.

"Open the fucking door, Drover," Peterson said.

"Told the truth for a change," Drover said, and replaced the receiver. He turned to open the door.

EIGHTEEN

G<small>ALLAGHER WAS</small> parked on Walton across from the Drake in a cab zone. The car was the kind of BMW that approachs forty thou, even when you get a deep discount. Drover didn't say a thing.

Gallagher took Michigan Avenue south toward the tall, boxy police headquarters building at Eleventh and State. The area south of the Loop is dingy even in daylight, even in summer when the streets are not clogged at the gutter lines with rotting snow.

First District was on the ground-floor side of headquarters on Eleventh Street.

"Don't I get handcuffs or something?" Drover broke the silence.

"You got a smart mouth," Tommy Gallagher said. "Why don't you shut up?"

Drover sat beside the policeman in the darkness. The car was parked in a no-parking zone across the street from the raucous post-midnight entrance of First District. A couple of hookers on teetery high heels were being marched on the slippery walk toward the glass doors. One slipped and fell, her short leather skirt slipping up to her panties. One of the arresting cops made a mock bow and extended his arm to help her up. If it was a her.

"Why'd you go to work on Leo Myers?" Drover said.

"Shut up," Gallagher said. He was watching his rearview mirror.

"What changed your mind about Dan Briggs?"

Silence.

"Peterson," Drover said.

Gallagher glanced at him. "Nobody'd believe your story except me. I guess I'm a gullible cop. You're doing all this as a favor for Fionna Givens. I bought that because the captain bought it and he was around when they invented the police star. He said you might be on the square."

"Did he? He never told me."

"You're a disappointment to him."

"Not like you."

"Not like me."

"Ah, the father I could have had," Drover said. "This is getting very sentimental."

"I talk to Leo the first time and then Peterson comes down on me. There's a federal investigation going on and it's bigger than you and me and bigger than Dan Briggs killing himself. Which, Peterson said, is probably what did not happen."

"You're telling me this."

"I'm telling you because I don't like to get pushed around by flyweights in suits from Uncle. I say to him, what about Dan Briggs and he says to me to just lay off Leo Myers. So I lay into Leo Myers instead."

"That's what I thought."

"I want to see how high this Peterson asshole can jump. He jumped high. He isn't thinking right. He wants me to bust you over anything that comes into my head, just to put the fear of God into you so you go away. But you won't go away, will you?"

The question was soft, almost shy.

"I was going to L.A. anyway," Drover said.

"Why's that?"

"See a man."

"What man was that?"

"Neil O'Neill. He dropped another bomb on his old friend and colleague Paul Givens. Something about a recruiting of a black player named Albert Brown."

"Which was nothing to do with Dan Briggs."

Drover thought about it. Gallagher was all bark and burrs, rough in the smooth places. He was the kind of guy who would never say "trust me" unless he didn't mean it. He hadn't said "trust me" to Drover.

"All right. I don't know. I ran a check on Dan Briggs last year. He was ref in four games involving St. Mary's and St. Mary's did not beat the spread in any one of them."

"That's a smoking gun, but in whose hands?"

"Players can shave games easier than refs, but you only have to fix one ref. A player goes on a cold streak, the coach can pull him, put in someone else isn't acting goofy. The ref is the ref."

"They watch each other."

"Like the way cops watch each other," Drover said.

Gallagher grunted. Drover had made his point.

"Neil O'Neill told the NCAA a little white lie about who recruited Albert Brown. I want to know why. I want to know what Neil O'Neill is hiding. He's hiding because he knows about this NCAA investigation and he isn't going on the air with it. Does that sound like a newsman to you?"

"Sounds like scum, which is the same thing."

"The press takes a bum rap," Drover said.

"Because they're mostly bums," the cop said.

"You watching for something in particular?"

"Peterson. He isn't going to follow through. The difference in being a cop and a G is that a G thinks his word is law and a cop knows different. I didn't get any respect from Peterson, and I guess I resent it."

"What are you going to do about Leo Myers?"

"Talk to his collector."

"Who is that?"

"You don't need to know, but what the hell. A guy named Bugs Rio. I talked to a guy who's supposed to know. Bugs Rio is collector for a guy named Steve March."

"And who's he?"

"He's a guy who works for another guy. All wise guys. Why did you see Tony Rolls?"

"Tony wanted to see me."

"What did he want?"

"He wanted to ask me the same questions that Peterson asked you—why are you hassling Leo Myers. For a two-bit book in a northwest side saloon, he has a lot of friends. If Tony is his friend, which I doubt."

"What'd you tell the greaseball?"

"Mr. Greaseball to you. I told him I don't know nothing."

"What'd he tell you?"

Jesus. It was a cold night and California dreaming was a million miles away. Drover shivered because the silent car was settling in with cold, like a front creeping across the prairies.

"Be careful. Cross at the corners. Watch for right-turning cars. Stuff like that."

"He's involved?"

"I honestly don't know but I honestly don't think so. But someone was onto me as fast as Peterson was onto you."

"Shit," Gallagher said. "I don't like to be ordered around by a geek in a suit. Okay. Peterson isn't going to show up."

"Drop me at the hotel to get my stuff."

"No. They might be watching it."

"Airport then. I can buy socks in L.A."

"And get clean underwear. You look scared enough to get it dirty," Gallagher said.

Drover stared out the window at the broken, bleak cityscape. "I get scared sometimes. Post-Vietnam-stress syndrome. I saw it on *Sally Jessy Raphaël*."

"Go back home and forget about this," Gallagher said.

Drover managed a smile then. "And let you get the girl?"

"I got girls. And an ex-wife."

"I've got to see this through," Drover said.

"Be stand-up."

"That's what it is. All that Catholic college education Captain Carmody paid for," Drover said.

"They still got flights out of O'Hare?"

"I don't know. Probably not. I can wait until morning."

"It's nearly two."

"I've stayed awake all night before," Drover said. And would again.

NINETEEN

NEIL O'NEILL and this one, this one was named Tammi or Bambi, they had done a couple of lines and were very wired for the sex act. The sex act was incredibly good. That's what Tammi or Bambi murmured before she dozed the way a dead person dozes. Then it was up and at 'em again and Neil O'Neill couldn't get enough of her. He had been like this all his life. There wasn't a woman worth looking at who wasn't worth pitching. He had his share of television groupies now because he was good-looking and a star on the most powerful medium in the universe, bigger than being president because you were part of their lives every goddamned day.

Tammi or Bambi was California golden, even all over her buttocks because the thong bikini was made for girls like her. Girl. Twenty? Neil couldn't tell ages that well anymore. A sign of getting older.

California morning was low and flat and cold. The rain was wetting down the creeping bent in Beverly Hills, Bel Air, and Westwood. Rain streaked the double-thick panes on the nineteenth floor of the Century Plaza, which boasted twenty-four-hour room service, starlets by the dozens, and a lobby where people went to be recognized.

Tammi or Bambi opened the door when he was in the shower. She thought it was room service with breakfast and thought it would be cute to open the door wearing his dress shirt over her nakedness. Everything about golden Tammi/Bambi was cute.

The guy was not dressed for room service. He wore a Bulls jacket picked up at O'Hare, a day's growth of beard, and the look of a tired man. He stared at her assets a moment and then said he had to see Neil.

"Who is it?" Neil said from the shower.

"Tell him I come from Fionna."

"Is that a name or something?" Tammi/Bambi said.

"A name."

"A guy from Fionna," she shouted.

"What?"

"Fionna," Drover said.

Neil walked into the bedroom with a towel around his waist and a scowl on his handsome face. "Who're you?"

"Drover. A friend of your wife's," Drover said. He looked at Neil's chest. Drover didn't think his own chest measured up. Neil was sleek, hairy, and kept himself up. Drover wondered what Fionna thought. Comparison-wise.

"My ex-wife."

"You're married?" squealed Tammi or Bambi. She must have done that before, the voice was practiced in its accusatory tone.

"Was," Neil said, blotting her out of the room. He had put the toke in the dresser drawer. The guy dressed like a narc. It made him nervous.

"Fionna and Paul."

"The Bobbsey Twins," Neil said, still not relaxing, the shower water beading on his chest. "What do you want?"

"A sit-down," Drover said. And took a chair. He stared at Tammi/Bambi's legs and wished the dress shirt weren't so long.

"This is a friend of mind, Tammi," Neil said suddenly.

"Bambi," Bambi said.

"Bambi," Neil said.

"Bambi. Like the deer," Drover said. "I thought that was a boy deer."

"I never met a boy named Bambi," Bambi said. The thought had never crossed her mind before. Possibly any thought.

"What do you want?"

"A sit-down. A chat. About you and the NCAA and the bells of St. Mary's. You know. Father O. The chapel building. The good old days," Drover said.

"Who are you exactly, besides some guy who needs a shave?"

"My name is Drover. I was in school when you were playing."

"Good for you."

"Just caught your senior year. You were terrific."

The soothing balm of a compliment always turned a talking head. Neil instinctively preened a moment and then realized he was standing in a towel, dripping on the carpet. He looked at Tammi. He meant Bambi. "Honey, get dressed, will you? I got to see this man."

"Why can't I stay?"

"Because I got to get ready for the game is why," Neil said. A man who had a lot of women in his life knew how to get rid of them. "You aren't her lawyer, are you?" he thought to ask.

"Do I look like a lawyer?"

"Then what are you?"

"Your conscience," Drover said.

Bambi pouted a bit because that was her habit and it looked cute. After she left, room service came up with coffee and rolls and orange juice. The rolls were flabby croissants, unflaky and unflattering. They just lay on the plate.

Drover poured himself coffee and took a roll and tore off a chunk. It was nearly noon in Chicago. He had been going for more than twenty-four hours, without sleep. O'Hare had been locked overnight to keep out the homeless, and he had spent the hours till his first flight riding the El back and forth from the airport to the end of the line in Forest Park. Subways were still for sleeping, as long as you put your trust in your fellow man.

"What about the NCAA?"

"You recruited Albert Brown."

"So what?"

"So why'd you tell the investigator, this Cary Lucas, you didn't? That it was Paul?"

"Paul did the lion's share of work. I gave him credit."

"Not at the time you signed Albert."

"That was then, this is now."

"Paul is getting shafted. Maybe starting with you."

"Paul was made to be shafted," Neil said. He poured coffee for himself. He was dressed now and looking sharp, the way he had always looked on the sidelines of the basketball courts he had dominated. Sort of roundball's version of Tom Landry.

"Fionna said he was being set up."

"You seeing Fionna. I thought she'd go into a convent when I left her."

"Nuns are getting scarce."

"Good. Maybe she's going to grow up."

"Like you are. Bambi is young enough to be your daughter."

"I'm not blessed with children. Maybe that's why I'm so fond of them."

"Why don't you do a commentary on what you know about the St. Mary's investigation?"

The question hung there.

Neil sipped his orange juice. "I'm thinking about it."

"What's to think about?"

"Who are you?"

"What did Lucas tell you? About the investigation?"

"He was looking into a recruiting violation. Allegation of one."

"He told you he was looking into point shaving by some members of St. Mary's."

Drover handed it to Neil. He was as cool as he was on television. He was famous for being cool when he was a coach. No towel biting or chair throwing, just cold and calm on the outside and pure ice water inside.

"Did he?"

"Look, Neil. I'll lay it out for you." Drover did in as few words as possible. About a dead ref named Dan Briggs who might have committed suicide. A bookie in Chicago. Anonymous notes to the board of governors and Paul Givens standing there holding the bag.

Neil let it sink in. He might have been listening to an inner voice.

The rain splattered against the windows and the wind rattled things.

"I didn't know about the ref. That was after my time."

"It might be coincidence, but in St. Mary's potential best year ever, bad stuff is going down."

"It happens that way. Coaching is like being in the lobster pot. You ever go down to Mexico, see the lobster pots? The lobsters keep crawling up to get out. You know why they don't? Because the other lobsters drag them back in. Nobody wants anybody to get too high. Maybe someone thinks Paul is getting too high too fast."

"It was your team. You gave it to him."

"I gave him what he wanted."

"The worst thing that can happen to a man is to get what he wants," Drover said.

"I got out in time," Neil said.

"I thought it was something like that."

Neil gave him a smile. Not the full voltage TV smile but a close cousin. "You met Dave Zekman?"

"I met him," Drover lied.

"Nice guy, huh?"

"Like what?"

"He came to St. Mary's from Santa Fe. Did a number down there."

"I follow sports. He's a gun for hire."

"A lot of athletic directors are now. They've got a program. They know more about maximizing profits than an investment banker. They're bean counters. I could smell him a mile off."

"And you thought it was time to git."

"He had a full plate the first couple of years, fucking with the football program. He couldn't alienate everyone at once. Just one at a time."

"But you saw the handwriting on the wall."

"Only a fool wouldn't. Or a fool like Paul Givens. Don't get me wrong. I like Paul. He's a good student of the game. He can see potential better than I can. He's got good eyes. And he can talk to the players. See. I can't talk to players anymore. I'm of the dinosaur Bobby Knight school or Ray Meyers. Or old Digger Phelps. I yell and scream. I believe in the work ethic. I wasn't ready for the not-my-job generation."

"And Paul is."

"Paul can deal because his heart is pure. Like his sister's."

"So Fionna's a chump too," Drover said. Very quietly.

Neil shook his handsome head. "Not a chump. A believer. Paul believes and it makes him a chump setup for someone like Dave Zekman. Who did he think brought Zekman in? Father George O'Brien. Everyone answers to someone. There are St. Mary's alums who want winners on the field, not good guys who play a fair game and shake hands at the end. They wouldn't care if we recruited a Libyan terrorist to do or die for Our Lady if we could win the Final Four."

"Father O was pushed into shaking up the A.D.?"

"I guessed something like that. Not one man or one group of men. But St. Mary's is a corporation and corporations have boards and they have to turn a buck. He was lackadaisical for too long about the athletic department. He brought in a shark, Dave Zekman, to shake it up and shake down the TV dollars."

"In the name of good, quality education."

Neil gave him the smile again. It was cynical, but it was so warm that you forgot the cold heart behind it, sort of the way Burt Lancaster managed to smile in *Elmer Gantry*.

"That's it, Fionna's friend. Put the illiterates on the front line, in the infantry, so that we can have more quality lawyers and doctors which we so desperately need."

"You started looking for another job the day Dave Zekman was named A.D.," Drover said.

"Right. Coaching, anything. I had a coaching offer or two. But then this came along. Money in a four-year contract. My Q profile was dazzling. That's what they said, they said people loved to watch me talk. Funny, I been doing it all my life and never got paid for it before."

"You set Paul up then."

"He set himself up. He wanted the job. I lobbied for him. Did Fionna tell you that? How about Paul?"

"Paul thinks you went to bat for him."

"I foxed that son of a bitch Zekman. I pitched Father O on loyalty, trust, all the bullshit, and he caved in. I could sell Judaism to Palestine if I wanted. Then I bid adieu."

"Walked out on your wife."

"It was over a long time, Drover. And I don't know exactly what you are to her, anyway."

"Friend. I went to school with her."

"You going to be more than a friend?"

"What about you, Neil?"

"I did the right thing. I gave her the house. She sold it and made a hundred grand. She's got a college education. She's going to trade school now, become a paralegal or legal secretary or something. She'll do all right. That part of my life is over. I don't have to explain it. Not to you, not to Fionna."

"Why did you lie about Paul? It brought me in all the way from Chicago."

"Go back to Chicago. I don't even know you."

"My name is Drover."

"That won't get you a free bus ride."

"I do work for an oddsmaker in Vegas and your name comes up. That's your team that Paul has. You recruited and trained it. Paul is going to reap the whirlwind with it. Are you lying because you want to distance yourself from the team? For the sake of your TV reputation?"

"TV reputation? A medium that gives you Jimmy the Greek and Valvono and Tarkanian has a reputation? I couldn't hurt myself if I tried."

"Neil. Somewhere in all this, a guy was killed."

"Is that right? What's that got to do with me?"

"A ref, a zebra. He worked games all over the Midwest. Even when you were coaching. Murder is different from a recruiting scandal."

"I didn't hear about a murder. I heard a zebra in Chicago killed himself."

They sized each other up in silence and Drover was found lacking because his clothes were wrinkled and slept-in and his face needed a shave. He didn't belong in this nice room with a tan face like Neil's and flabby croissants on china. It suddenly dawned on him.

He got up from the cart table and looked down at Neil.

"You going to divorce her?"

"It looks that way."

"Paul said he hoped you'd come back together."

"Paul would say that. Even believe it. Funny to think he'd talk to a stooge for a bookie in Vegas."

"I'm not a stooge, Neil. And Paul's turned me in to the NCAA already I'm sure. His heart is pure."

"Yeah, I know."

"See you around the gambling tables."

"I don't gamble," Neil said.

"You're gambling now."

Neil looked at him.

"Just don't crap out," Drover said.

TWENTY

Bugs Rio wiped at his watery eyes and lit a cigarette. His thirtieth of the day, and it was only the middle of the afternoon. Steve March was in his office. The cheap panel walls were littered with neat rows of framed photographs showing Chicago sports legends. This was A. B. Sportsmarketing, Inc. They were into T-shirts, it said somewhere. Also sports caps, very big. The one-story brick building was on Foster Avenue, almost at the tip of the northwest suburbs. A. B. Sportsmarketing was as phony as the paneling.

"The guy is registered at the Drake but he called up from California to hold his room. He's in Vegas now. He was in L.A. This cost me a few beans."

"Good, Bugs," Steve March said. "But I wanted to know his clout."

"He don't have none that I know of. He's supposed to be messing around because of something someone asked him. The ex-wife of Neil O'Neill on TV. She goes by Fionna Givens and she's got a rat apartment around DePaul University, studio. She's a busybody. She told this Drover guy about the NCAA, about this zebra killing himself because he was fixing games."

Steve March let a smile out of its cage. It wasn't a friendly one.

"She humping with Drover?"

"I dunno. He starts snooping around after she talked to him, got him stirred up. Now I hear, but this isn't a fact, that he even talked to Paul Givens."

"The guy is all over the place."

"Yeah," said Bugs. He wasn't comfortable at all. For some reason, Steve March had the air conditioner in the wall on. It sent out a steady stream of outside air pulled in by the fan and it battled with the heat banging up from the floor ducts. Very strange man, Bugs thought for the ninety-ninth time. Very much into psychological problems.

"How you get all this stuff on Drover?"

"I talked around. I went by this saloon, Maguire's. Big beefy guy named Black Kelly, he said I could get hold of Drover at the Drake. Said he was registered there. This Kelly was a fireman once in town, retired out to California."

"So who cares? What about Drover?"

"I call the Drake, get connected with his room. Then I get no answer. I go over and talk to a guy in the union works there, he gets me the answers. About California, he said he was in California but that he'd be back in a day or so and they should hold the room. Then I get into his room. A guy I know works there. There's a bag there but the bed ain't been slept in. Then the guy for a dollar tells me this cop named Gallagher, the same Gallagher, he and Drover left the hotel together. That's when I tried Vegas and he was there, talking to this Fox Vernon guy."

"You could of been a detective or something," Steve March said. He was smiling the same smile at Bugs, a dreamy kind of smile.

"Where's Fionna Givens or whatever?"

"I dunno. Maybe going to school, she's got classes at DePaul. I dunno. Maybe home."

"What's she look like?"

"Black hair, long, Irish face, you know."

"I don't know, that's why I ask. So. All this is about one cheap cop and an asshole with no connections from Vegas. And some busy-body girl. Fuck them."

"What'd we do?"

"The cop. Gallagher? He got a connection?"

"Was a protégé of Captain Carmody, you remember."

"Big Mick asshole, he killed Frankie Deanno in the fifties, I remember that like I remember yesterday. He was in the Murder Squad, he liked to muscle us."

"He's out of it. An old man."

"Yeah? Is that what you think, Bugs? An old man calls on his boy to help this Drover out."

"He knew Drover. Knew his family."

"Drover got family?"

"Just this fat Irish guy, Kelly, friend of his. And Carmody."

Steve March picked up a matchbook imprinted with the name of the company and did a toothpick on his incisors with it. He was thinking.

Bugs squirmed the way he always did. Sit-downs with Steve were never pleasant, even when he was being nice.

"I don't wanna mess with no cops, not even retired cops. I don't know how to reach out and touch Drover, at least not now. What do you think I should do?"

"You gotta do something?"

"I gotta do something. There's things and things you don't know are in my head. Trust me. I gotta do something."

"Whaddaya gotta do?"

"What's her name again, Fionn?"

"Fionna Givens."

"Irish name. They all got these asshole names now. My cousin was going to call his kid Sean, try to make him sound Irish. Sounds like a shine name to me."

Bugs tried to make a smile.

"Whaddaya think this Fionna knows about anything?"

"I don't think she knows nothing."

"She told Drover that Briggs didn't kill himself."

"I don't know that. Drover might have figured that out."

"He can't figure nothing out. There's a fucking police report of suicide, that's all that's there," Steve March said. He was still smiling at Bugs and Bugs had given up trying to match it back.

"So whaddaya gonna do, Steve?"

"I'm gonna put the fear on somebody."

Bugs stared.

"Drover?" he said.

"Maybe. He's a straight geek. No connections."

"We gotta wait till he gets in town. We got nobody we can talk to for that kind of work in Vegas."

"Yeah, I know."

"Then we wait on him?"

"Naw." Steve was jiggling his right leg, getting ready to scooter his Park Avenue some place. It was the jittery time of day. He pushed himself up from his swivel chair. "You did good, Bugs. Drover's got no clout I can see. So maybe we just could let it ride. Except it bothers me. Besides, I could go over and talk to this broad and see what she's made of."

"Jesus, Steve. Why do that?"

"Because she can tell me what she knows. And then I know what Drover knows and what Drover told the cop. And then I can tell her one of two things."

Bugs waited.

"Tell her to not go sticking her nose in business," Steve said.

And Bugs didn't want to hear the other thing.

TWENTY-ONE

THE BOMBSHELL came down at 4:00 P.M. eastern time, right out of the NCAA board of governors office. The rumors, so far unprinted, were true, the unidentified spokesman told the Associated Press. "St. Mary's College in North Fork, Indiana, is under investigation for possible recruiting violations." Nothing more than that. Under Neil O'Neill or Paul Givens? No comment. About whom? About a present player. Who? Figure it out. It wasn't much, only enough for a sports page headline in every paper in the country and a line on the *NBC Nightly News* and *ABC Evening News*. *CBS News* skipped it because of a four-part series on the dangers of braces.

The very next thing you knew, Paul Givens was giving a press conference in the athletic building of St. Mary's College. It was 8:00 P.M. central time, and it was snowing hard again so that only sixty or so correspondents, cameramen, and TV crewmen showed up.

"Allegations of illegal recruiting procedures have been circulated by the NCAA," Paul Givens said. He was reading from a handwritten script. "As far as I know, there have been no recruiting violations. But these and other rumors circulating about the conduct of the coaching staff of St. Mary's College have had a deleterious effect on the team and I think it is unfair, unfair for the players and the fans and the alumni who support St. Mary's. I have nothing to hide and nothing to say to the charges until I see them specifically. But for a number of reasons, I think it is in the best interest of the St. Mary's Bulldogs that I temporarily step aside as head coach and turn the reins over to my first assistant, a fine coach, Tom Dressler."

The questions piled on, and Dave Zekman watched the whole thing from his closed-door office down the hall. Officially, he was out of town. Paul Givens was supposed to dangle in the wind alone on this one. He was doing a teary-eyed stand-up job.

Dave Zekman said aloud, "See, he cries. That isn't a head coach, not by a long shot." He was speaking to no one but himself. And he was smiling because his judgment of Paul Givens's character had finally been confirmed.

TWENTY-TWO

Fox Vernon usually started early in the day, around noon, and retired after the supper hour for a few hours' sleep, to be up and about again around eleven at night. He was on Vegas time, set to an internal clock because gambling dens did not have clocks.

This was his early shift, six at night, and he and Drover had watched the proceedings at St. Mary's live on an intercepted NBC feed to local affiliates that is obtainable with sophisticated satellite-interception equipment.

When it was over, Vernon left the monitor on but punched the mute button.

He and Drover were in the plain, bare-walled office Vernon called home behind the Shamrock Casino Hotel. The big outer room was full of cubicles containing computers and men and women who knew how to crunch sports numbers and follow the shifting sports lines as surely as stock market traders track the Dow. Fox Vernon was a benevolent, hands-on boss whose only rule was that no one working for him gamble and no one put any sports paraphernalia on the walls to show some hometown allegiance. Sports was business, nothing to relax about. Behind his back, he was called Headmaster.

"If he isn't guilty of something, why did he do it?"

"He was born guilty," Drover said. He had shaved, showered, and shampooed since breakfast in L.A. with Neil O'Neill. "Original sin. Someone tipped him over the edge. Maybe it was me."

"Oh. So you were born guilty too, huh?" Fox Vernon tapped his fingertips together and leaned back in the lazy swivel chair at the computer. His glass of ginger ale was by his side. It was as strong as it went for him.

"The plate has too much on it. It's overkill. The NCAA first had a dead ref. Then it had allegations of point shaving. Finally it gets a recruiting scandal. This makes St. Mary's sound like UNLV without morals."

"It's a bit much. No wonder the NCAA only threw out the recruiting thing. The ref is dead. No point in attacking the integrity of a dead zebra. It reflects on all the zebras. College refs are just too many, too part-time, too tenuous. They need to professionalize it."

"What are you going to do? Have a thousand nationally certified refs for every game from East Podunk Teachers College to Georgetown?" Drover said. "It's the economics of college sports. Pay no one but pile up the money from TV and the sneaker manufacturers."

"And we thought all this had been abolished by the Thirteenth, Fourteenth, and Fifteenth amendments. Slavery, I mean," Fox Vernon said.

"You don't have to talk down to me. I went to college."

"Sorry. You're younger than I am. And you went to an inferior school."

"We can't all be University of Chicago grads."

"True," Fox Vernon said, with satisfaction. His various degrees wore frames on the walls in his apartment. He even wore a maroon sweatshirt when jogging, a reminder to him of the days when amateur athletics were left to amateurs.

"Red herrings," Drover said. It had been nagging him all day. And now it had exploded in his mind with the resignation—or whatever it was—of Paul Givens as head coach of St. Mary's.

"Beg your pardon?"

"Too many things. I put them all together in my mind. I should have stuck to skepticism, the old reporter's best tool. I must be getting rusty."

"Rusty about who or what?"

"There are separate problems here. Recruiting. Was Albert Brown recruited in a way to break the NCAA rules? There's every possibility of that. Albert doesn't seem to know because Albert, like so many players, will not be working on the next Titan rocket program. Neil O'Neill may know, but he won't tell, and besides, he doesn't give a shit. Problem two: Did players shave points? All I get is that this NCAA guy talked to the players once and let it go. That's the old in and out when the NCAA doesn't believe something too hard. And what about the dead zebra? Is that a third problem or is it tied to the other two? See what I mean?"

"One plus one plus one doesn't add up," Fox Vernon said.

"I think Dave Zekman was after Paul Givens because I believe Neil O'Neill and because we have his record as a program changer and headhunter down at Santa Fe. Maybe the pressure of it all got to Paul and he really honestly thinks the team is better off without him for now."

"What is solid, absolutely solid, is a dead referee named Dan Briggs."

"Except there's an FBI guy named Peterson who doesn't want me to bother about it."

"Maybe he has a loftier agenda," Fox Vernon said. He wasn't trying to be funny.

"But how do I find out what it is?"

"Maybe you don't. Your . . . contact with the Outfit is warning you off. Stay warned. Stay in California with Kelly and eat carcinogens in ground meat."

"Sure."

They sat there, waiting for words of inspiration. The TV monitor was showing the remains of a Duke basketball game played at an absurdly early hour so the network could pack in a doubleheader. Sports was for gluttons.

The telephone rang. Not the rinnggg of America but the ding of European phones. Fox punched a button and picked up the receiver.

"He's here."

He handed over the phone.

Drover always expected bad news on a telephone. He was seldom disappointed.

"Me," Black Kelly said. His voice was sober and subdued.

"Yeah?"

"Someone scared Fionna," Kelly said.

"Scared her?"

"Say beat her up."

"Where the hell are you?"

"I'm at Grant Hospital. She's all right if you call a broken rib and two black eyes and a cheekbone fracture all right."

The sick feel churned up, and Drover made a noise to gulp it down.

"My sister called me when Fionna called her. I came over but I can't see her yet. They told me about it, the paramedics when I came in. I knew one of the guys." Kelly always knew someone. Maybe four thousand people in Chicago and half the population of Santa Cruz. Drover trusted everything he said.

"You got to ask her what it was about."

"She told my sister to get me. To tell you to drop it, to not do anything more. Stay away, she told my sister before she hung up. Message for you. 'Stay away, this is bad.' "

"All right," Drover said. "I'll be there as soon as I can."

"Don't go to your fucking hotel, for Christ's sake," Kelly said. He rarely used bad language. "You got another place?"

"I got another place. How do I reach you?"

"Call my sister. I'll be at the hospital, then I'll be some place else, I'm going to talk around." Kelly talked around the way detectives do it. He could always find things out, even when he didn't know what he was looking for.

"Stay away from the book in Glasses. Leo Myers. There's bad feel about him."

"Anything else?"

"Yeah, there's something else. You know cops?" Drover said.

"I know cops, judges, lawyers, you name it. You work for the city, you get to know everyone," Kelly said.

"You know this cop named Tom Gallagher? A loo from Central Division, I don't know, planning department or something."

"I don't know the name. Would he be related to Jimmy Gallagher?"

"I don't know who he's related to, Kelly. I got a ride with him to the police station last night. Seems a million years ago. Very nice car. BMW. The police don't use BMWs, do they?"

"Cops use what they get. He might have got the car from a drug sale. When the druggists are convicted, their shit is seized and sold at auction. He might have got in on a good car."

That disappointed Drover. He really thought he had something there.

"But I can ask around," Kelly said.

"Yeah. But keep your head down, Black."

"I always do. Make sure you do the same."

"Tell Fionna . . ." He let it go.

"Yeah. I'll make up something."

He held the receiver in his hand a moment longer than the connection demanded.

"What's going on?" Fox Vernon said when Drover replaced the receiver.

Drover turned. "Someone beat up Fionna and warned me off."

"Like I did a moment ago."

"Fuck both of you."

"Drover, Drover," Fox said.

"I got nothing, and yet everything is suddenly coming against me. Against Fionna. I want to talk to that NCAA guy so bad that I'd buy a ticket to get in."

"But a ticket then. Why wouldn't he talk to you?"

"Because someone in the NCAA is playing games and maybe

he's part of it. I don't know what the game is but something is going on that's bad, very bad. What do you know about him, Cary Lucas?"

"He was a police detective in Minneapolis. He went to the NCAA four years ago. Played some football at Minnesota but he was too small."

"Good," Drover said. "I want him small enough to whack around."

"Drover, you can't get involved like that."

Drover picked up the telephone and dialed a long-distance number. He waited. When the priest came on the line, he said, "Hello, Father O'Brien? This is Danforth. Roger Danforth with the board of governors. Yes, that's right, did we meet at the Four last year? No, but I look forward to it. Father, I wanted to keep you abreast and I need a favor—yes, I saw it, I think that was not necessary but it's best for you to judge about the good of the game, of the team, I . . . yes, yes, Father I was wondering if you would be so kind as to give me the number for Cary Lucas. The office is closed and something has come up and he's on the road and I don't have a clue as to where he . . . yes, I'll wait."

They both waited.

"Yes. Oh, I see, he's staying in Charlotte tonight. Good. Good. Goood. Thank you. No, Father, I really can't comment but I don't want you to worry. St. Mary's is an example to many of us of how to run a fine, upstanding athletic program and I'm sure we can clear up the discrepancies. I really think that Mr. Givens was premature in . . . Yes."

Drover looked at Fox.

"Oh yes, Mr. Zekman's advice. Yes. I suppose you have to do what is best for you and for your fine school. Yes. Yes. Thank you and I will stay in touch and thank you for your help, it's very embarrassing for a member of the board to not know where . . . No, it doesn't involve St. Mary's, Father, we're investigating other matters as well. We leave no stone unturned. Yes. Well, between us, and I hope you keep it in strictest confidence, it's something at Illinois. Yes. Thank you again. Good night, Father. God bless."

Fox looked at him. "The God bless was gratuitous. Your cultured accent was acceptable, though."

"So was the Illinois stuff gratuitous. Be all over by next week. I never liked the Illini," Drover said.

"You can be mean."

Drover stared right thorugh the mild man in the swivel chair. "Wait till you see me in Charlotte."

TWENTY-THREE

THE MOON made the top side of the clouds look like bundles of wool spread out in a carpet all the way from Los Angeles International to O'Hare in Chicago. Drover thought he would sleep but didn't. He inhaled all of *Time, Newsweek,* and parts of *Forbes*—the parts he understood. The flight attendant in first class was named Pamela, and she wanted to know about Drover in a roundabout way. He decided to tell her he was a brain surgeon. She didn't believe him.

It was ten minutes to midnight Chicago time when he walked through the jetway into terminal four. The vastness of the airport buildings under fluorescence made the case against the future and brave new world. Drover dropped a quarter into the first phone he found and got Maguire's on the third ring. Kelly answered it himself.

"She's fine, fine," he said. "They did what they had to do and sedated her. The cops talked to her and she couldn't tell them much of anything except what the guy looked like. A big, dark-haired guy with eyes the colors of olives. Green olives. Swarthy. The cops seem to take it with a grain of salt, they wanted to know if she was living with someone, stuff like that. Don't you love cops?"

"Yeah," Drover said to himself. He promised to see Kelly sometime.

"Where you going?"

"Charlotte. First plane out in the morning."

"What's in Charlotte?"

"See a man," Drover said.

"You wouldn't want to tell me?"

"I'll tell you when I see how it goes."

Captain Carmody opened the door of his flat and stared at Drover a moment, then turned his back and went into the kitchen. Same as before. The flat had a timeless quality as though everything was under glass and waiting for a museum.

"You want a drink?"

"I want to flop. I'll be out in the morning."

"What was you saying on the phone about the hotel?"

"I thought someone would have brought you up to date by now," Drover said. He sat down at the kitchen table and placed folded hands on the oilcloth.

"Date about what?"

"Your protégé, Tommy Gallagher. The cop who was a stand-up guy," Drover said.

Carmody said nothing. His eyes were hard because forty-six years in the street had made them that way. When you've seen and heard everything, you lose your sense of sight and sound.

"Stand-up Gallagher took a run at a small-time bookie named Leo Myers. Myers does business in a neighborhood saloon called Glasses on Irving Park. He was Dan Briggs's book."

"So Briggs was doing naughty things," Carmody said. He grunted and stared at his whiskey bottle. Sure. Why not? He picked up the squarish bottle and poured a measure and looked at Drover. Drover shook his head: He didn't have time for a bourbon hangover in the morning.

"Briggs was killed," Drover said.

"Ah. You're a detective now. How do you deduce that?"

"A G-man named Peterson gave something along that line to Gallagher but Gallagher was supposed to back off. Instead, Gallagher went after Leo Myers about Briggs' being whacked instead of committing suicide and Peterson put a collar on him. Why? Because Peterson must have something in mind for Leo Myers that is more important than a case of murder."

"You tell wonderful stories, it's a shame you don't still work for the papers. I like my fiction, read the papers every day," Carmody said.

"Remember why I came to you? Remember Fionna Givens? Well, someone beat the shit out of her tonight."

Carmody put down his glass. Nothing dramatic, just setting the glass on the table. "Is that a fact?"

"She's in Grant Hospital. A broken bone or two. Whoever beat her up told her to stop messing around with this matter. Told her to tell me to go back to California and leave this thing alone. Now, what thing would that be? Looking into point shaving by players? Then why beat up Fionna Givens?"

"Give you a warning," Carmody said.

"Sure. Scare me by showing what they're willing to do to her. Nice guys. What kind of a guy beats up women?"

"When the stakes are big enough, they can butcher babies if they have to," Carmody said. "It has to be important. They're animals."

"So it's important, Captain. So what are you going to do about it?"

Carmody said, "I suddenly owe you something?"

"Yeah. You owe me a flop on your couch tonight, and tomorrow morning you call up your protégé and you ask him what the hell is going on. Light a fire under him before someone comes after me."

"So you're scared."

Carmody was smiling.

"I'm scared. Especially when I don't know who's doing what to who for what reason. Some guy beats up Fionna and then tells her it's a warning to me, that scares me."

"And that's why you can't go back to your hotel."

"Among other reasons." Drover looked at his hands and decided to rearrange them on the table. Satisfied, he said, "Captain. This is deeper than I thought it was going to be. Ask a couple of questions for an old girlfriend."

Carmody nodded, to himself and his glass. "Tommy Gallagher is a straight shooter. If he's onto something, he'll stay with it."

"You been watching *Dragnet* reruns, Cap. This is real life in real time. Cops get kinky or they get warned off something. Peterson warned off Tommy Gallagher and he might tell you why and what this is about."

"The only reason I'll do anything is because someone beat up that girl. Fionna. I'll go just that far to find out why. Does Tommy Gallagher know she was beat up?"

"I don't know. It won't make the papers or anything, I doubt it'll be in the daily police bulletin. I don't know."

"Well, I'll tell him for a start."

"I'm going to call a cab order. I got a flight out at six-fifteen."

"Use United-American. I know the dispatch, a guy named Reedy," Captain Carmody said.

Drover shook his head. "I never seen such a town for connections. Even in simple matters. You can't order a cab without using influence."

"Don't put on airs, kid."

Drover stared at the large, old man.

"After all, what was I to you but another connection?"

TWENTY-FOUR

"WHAT CAN I do for you, Mr. Briggs?"

Drover stirred cream into his coffee. The coffee shop in the Holiday Inn was bright, chirpy, and cute. They always were. The only difference in Holiday Inns is the people and Charlotte people are warm, Southern, all smiles and biscuits and gravy, and "you wan' 'nother one, sugar?"

Cary Lucas looked Minnesota from the top of his corn silk through his lake-blue eyes to the cleft in his chin and his farmer's hands. But he had the wary smile of a cop waiting for the con.

"My father is what," Drover said. "He killed himself for no reason and left a typewritten note that explained nothing and all I get from the NCAA is that there is an ongoing investigation and I'm fed up."

"I'm sorry for your loss," Cary Lucas said. Still sitting there like a cat waiting to pounce.

"Okay. But that doesn't give me satisfaction. My father never fixed a game in his life."

"Your father was a gambler. He gambled on games. Illegally," Cary Lucas said.

"Is there any other way to gamble? Other than living in Nevada? He loved basketball." The funny thing was that Drover was working into the part of Dan Briggs's aggrieved son. His eyes were haggard, and that was no act, just the fact of not getting much sleep in the last forty-eight hours spent in several different time zones. He felt the part of Dan Briggs's son was really in his bones. "I went down to St. Mary's and had a long talk with Father George O'Brien, and I think you people are just building up a case on nothing. You got an anonymous letter—more than one anonymous letter—and you're constructing all this investigation or whatever you call it on that, and all I know is that my father is dead."

"We didn't kill him," Lucas said. He hadn't touched his biscuits and gravy. Drover had walked in on him after he had ordered and demanded the interview. If this was an interview.

"I want to know who did."

Cary Lucas stared right through him then.

"You want to say something?" Drover said.

"Mr. Briggs. I can tell you that what I'm doing for the NCAA has nothing to do with your father. I don't know why your father died, but it had nothing to do with us."

It startled Drover so that he forgot his next question. They shared the silence in the clattering room. Neither made a move.

"You saying that you aren't looking into my father's death? That there is no investigation?" Drover realized he was blathering because he couldn't figure out what this revelation meant.

"I'm saying I talked to him once. About certain allegations. We went over the points, one by one. And your father was cooperating with me. He said he had heard rumors inside the conference of a ref getting fixed and he had his own ideas about it. He said he would look around. I said he should share any suspicions with me and he said he'd get back to me. This was on a Monday. He killed himself on Wednesday and left that note."

"Then why did he kill himself?"

"You should ask someone else that."

"Like who?"

"I can't say," Cary Lucas said. He looked pained. Maybe he was the one cop in a thousand with a heart. "I appreciate what this is doing to you," he said.

"Who should I ask? You can tell me that. I'm sitting here bleeding."

"I think you should go to the authorities and ask them to look into the suicide and maybe see if they're . . . well, if they're making another judgment, maybe pursuing another line of thought."

"Like what?"

"Look, Mr. Briggs, I'm not at liberty to tell you anything. I don't know very much anyway. I just know that as for the NCAA, we're not interested in your father's . . ." He let it go because Drover had made his eyes show pain. Drover thought the guy did have a heart and Drover was ready to stomp on it.

"I think you should go to the FBI," Cary Lucas said. "Only I didn't tell you that. I just think that you should ask someone else."

"The FBI?"

"That's more than I should have said."

Drover saw it was. This was no put-on. The guy was feeling sorry for the son of Dan Briggs and it made Drover a little bit ashamed.

"Do they know something? Do they know my father didn't kill himself?"

"I don't know, Mr. Briggs. I know that when I talked to your father, it was straightforward. I said we had information that he was wagering on games with a bookmaker in Chicago and he denied it. I didn't have proof, only the rumors. There was a bookmaker and he had a name but no one stepped forward to make a charge against your father. We're not running an inquisition, Mr. Briggs. Do you know how many allegations get handled every year? Hundreds. We're swamped sometimes. Sports is big business and we all know it. Money attracts greed. I think it was simpler for me when I was just a cop in Minneapolis, dealing with ordinary scum."

That surprised Drover. He saw through the wary cop eyes and saw that Cary Lucas had never expected to find alligators in the sewers working for the NCAA.

"Did St. Mary's break any rules?" Drover said.

Too far. The cop in Lucas went cold. "That isn't even going to get a 'mind your own business.' "

"I felt sympathy for Father O'Brien when I talked to him. He's terribly upset. His coach resigned last night."

"I know."

"Because of the NCAA," Drover said.

Now the lake-blue eyes were frozen solid and the freeze went deep enough so that the ice fishermen could truck out their shanties.

"The NCAA announced a investigation because there were rumors and some of the rumors were wrong," Cary Lucas said. "We wanted to lift the cloud."

"What cloud?"

Cary Lucas didn't say the interview was ended but Drover thought it might be true.

"The cloud about point shaving by players? You didn't announce anything about that."

Cary Lucas let the silent stare do the talking.

"You've got a single thing out of this, don't you? You've got a recruiting violation. There's enough there to go public with it, warn St. Mary's that the hammer is coming down," Drover said.

"Who are you?" Quietly and politely in a soft Minnesota accent that is usually heavy with civility.

"Who do you think?"

"You aren't Briggs."

"I lied," Drover said.

"You son of a bitch," Cary Lucas said.

"More coffee?"

Neither man nodded.

"Y'all want more coffee, sugar?"

Drover nodded then to get rid of her. She poured for him and, still smiling, stared at Cary Lucas. "How 'bout you?"

"All right," Cary Lucas said.

She dropped the check on the table and walked away, her right hand clutching the requisite two glass coffee pots, orange-rimmed for decaf and brown-rimmed for regular.

"My name is Drover," Drover said.

"I don't really give a damn."

"A woman named Fionna Givens O'Neill asked me to look around for her. Her brother is Paul Givens. Her ex-husband-to-be is Neil O'Neill."

"So you're some kind of private dick? I hate P.I.s more than street scum."

"I know what you mean," Drover said. "No, not a P.I. A friend. I knew Fionna. The first thing struck me was that Dan Briggs did not kill himself. Over what? An allegation, an anonymous allegation that might lead to dismissal from a part-time job? Come on."

"There could have been criminal charges."

"Sure, like the point-shaving thing in New York State a few years ago. Sure there could have, but it was a long way from what you tell me you were talking to Briggs about and where some D.A. was going to hotdog a prosecution. No, I didn't like it then, and I like it less now."

"My feelings about you exactly."

"And I thought I was being charming by being so forthcoming," Drover said. "Well, let's drop the charm then, Cary. I think you couldn't find your ass with a flashlight and a map. That's for starters."

"I think you ought to make it finishers."

"The FBI for its own reasons wants you and your masters to stop snooping around a corpse named Briggs and you're only too happy to because the NCAA doesn't want to know about crooked zebras in the first place. So you happily pursue a mere investigation of St. Mary's basketball team on the basis of . . . what? Two bits of anonymous information. Point shaving? Recruiting violations in signing up Albert Brown? Which is it? It isn't both, I know that."

"You do? What a bright boy." Cary had turned all street cop, mean and ready to slam a head against a door.

"You asshole, I'm not playing with you," Drover said. "Fionna got beat up last night by some guy who warned her to stay away from the NCAA investigations and to tell me to do the same. The guy hit her hard enough to break bones and put her in the hospital. So what does that make you, Cary? I don't really care if you like me or not because I am coming after you and the NCAA and anyone else who's been faking this and that. One guy is dead and one woman is in a hospital and cops get scared off asking questions and the NCAA kisses the FBI's ring."

"You a newspaperman?"

"Yeah. *Los Angeles Times.*"

"What's your name again?"

"Skip it, Cary."

"How'd you find me?"

"I told you. I talked to Father O at St. Mary's."

"Who were you then?"

"Danforth on your board of governors."

Cary Lucas stared but the eyes were melting. To Drover's surprise, he smiled. "You're a sneaky bastard, aren't you?"

"No. Just a born liar," Drover said. "But this is the truth, Cary, and I'm telling you because I like you: Two nights ago in Chicago I was visited by a guy named Peterson with the FBI who wants me to stop messing with a bookie named Leo Myers. He is very federal about this and does the booga-booga on me."

"Go ahead."

"Then last night Fionna gets beat up and is given the same message."

"You think the FBI beat her up?"

"No. I think there are just too many people who don't want anyone to look into the death of Dan Briggs. So I fly to Charlotte to see what you think and you tell me that the damned NCAA was warned off going further on its Briggs investigation. Now, what do you think of that?"

"I didn't know all this."

"You don't know half of it," Drover agreed.

"I don't like to be set up."

"No one does."

"You going to print any of this?"

"No. This is my vacation. I'm doing a favor for a friend who is in Grant Hospital in Chicago at the moment. A nice girl I knew a long time ago."

"I didn't want the board to make any announcement," Cary Lucas said. "Shows how much influence I have."

"You've got something?"

"I've got something."

"What is it?"

"I can't tell you."

"Neil O'Neill gave Albert Brown's mama four hundred dollars for a new dishwasher."

"Along those lines."

"That's chickenshit."

"Chickenshit, as you say."

"So Albert is in trouble and Paul Givens is in trouble and St. Mary's gets slapped with a black eye and for what? For a fucking dishwasher?"

"It wasn't a dishwasher. I said it was along those . . . monetary lines."

"And you don't do a thing about a dead zebra in Chicago who got dead from someone else's hand."

"I don't know that. What I know is that I was told to drop this thing and the board agreed to drop it."

"And the point shaving by the team. That's bullshit too?"

"Apparently," Cary Lucas said. "I don't get anywhere on it. We used a computer, studied game films, checked with people in the . . . gambling establishment."

Drover let that one pass.

"So what you've got is a single recruiting violation done by a guy who is safe and away on network television and couldn't give a shit less about what you find out about him."

"It happens that way sometimes," Cary Lucas said.

"But where did the tips come from?"

"I don't know."

"What were they? On paper? Tape?"

"I can't tell you that."

"When did you get them?"

"Most of this stuff dribbled in around last May."

"But not the stuff about Dan Briggs's maybe fixing games," Drover said.

"No. That was separate."

"Why put these things together then?"

"I didn't put them together. Dan Briggs worked the Midwest, he

165

did some St. Mary's games in the past few years. And then we get tips about St. Mary's doing bad things and we have to look for them."

"What are you going to do, Cary?"

Cary stared at him for a long moment. The room was emptying out. The waitresses were standing at their station, talking about tips, hairdos, and raising kids.

"Do what I'm paid to do."

"St. Mary's can win the Four this year."

"They well might."

"When will this come down?"

"After the postseason tournament. We won't interfere before then, I don't think."

"What happens to St. Mary's?"

"First-time violation. I don't know. I don't decide these things."

"Don't do it. Paul Givens doesn't deserve it."

"Yeah. I liked him. He seemed like a decent guy. I don't know, maybe he was too much of a Boy Scout but a decent guy."

"What's wrong with being a Boy Scout? Honor God and country."

"I wouldn't figure you were a Scout admirer."

"Paul doesn't deserve this, Albert doesn't deserve this. And neither does St. Mary's."

"I do what I have to do," Cary Lucas said.

"You're a Boy Scout yourself."

Cary looked at his cup and then looked up. "The FBI guy was named Peterson. Out of Chicago. Same as your guy. I don't really know what they're messing with but they want the NCAA to stay the hell away from Dan Briggs and Leo Myers and whoever else they might have led to."

"I'm going to rattle cages," Drover said.

"Go get 'em."

"You got any idea who sent you all this bad stuff about St. Mary's?"

"Maybe."

"Maybe means you know."

"Maybe means maybe."

"Who is the maybe?"

"I can't say. And if I can't be certain, I don't want to say."

"But you don't mind dropping the bomb yesterday that panicked

Paul Givens into quitting as coach. Paul is convinced that he's the reason the Bulldogs lost the other night to Penn State, that the team is losing confidence in him the longer this NCAA investigation continues."

"I didn't do that."

"Who did it?"

"I don't know. It was a decision a level above me. I'm just a guy in the field."

"It stinks."

"Bad things happen sometimes."

"A couple of hundred bucks to some poor old black lady in North Carolina and you bring all this down."

"Don't do the crime if you can't do the time."

"Sure. Who's going to do time? Neil O'Neill? Last time I saw him, he was having breakfast in his suite at the Century Plaza Century City near Santa Monica with an underdressed groupie named Bambi. He's really going to be hurting. Hurting is what Fionna Givens is doing right now in a hospital. Hurting is Paul giving up his team."

"You should have considered being a lawyer," Cary Lucas said.

"I write too well."

Cary said, "I'm going to be here today, maybe tomorrow."

"You want me to stay in touch," Drover said.

"Well, I'd kind of like to see how this turns out, when you start rattling cages. I like to see the animals get stirred up. Mean streak in me I rarely show," Cary Lucas said.

For the first time, Drover grinned.

Cary Lucas was nodding.

The grin spread.

"You ain't seen nothin' yet," Drover said.

TWENTY-FIVE

Leo Myers got into the BMW waiting outside his apartment on Kedvale. It was too early in the morning for him and he showed it. His face was full of gray stubble and his eyes were not their right color.

"Jesus, It's the earliest I been up since I was in the Army," Leo said.

"Which country you fight for? Musta been the losing side," Tommy Gallagher said, and started up. They were driving no place and Leo knew this was a command performance.

In Decmeber, the forest preserves in and around Chicago are usually empty and beautiful. The vast nature preserves are usually selected as the places to hold public trysts and private conversations. The preserve on Foster Avenue was called Bessemer Woods and there were only a couple of cars parked in the lot, and beyond was the winding drive that led deeper into forest and field.

Leo Myers was scared because it was all so private all of a sudden. Not like meeting in a restaurant or on the street.

Tommy Gallagher put the car in "park" and turned to Leo. He wasn't smiling or scowling or anything. The cop's face was just terrifingly blank.

"Leo, who you working for?"

"You know who I work for. I pay the tax."

"I ain't talking about Bugs Rio. I want to know who you're working for."

"I don't know what you mean."

That's when Tommy took out the pistol. A .357 Colt Python with the short barrel looks like a cartoon gun because it is so big.

"See, I won't kill you in my car because I couldn't stand the stains, but you get maybe three or four feet away, I can make your head look like a cantaloupe was dropped from the top of the Sears Tower."

"Jesus, Tommy, what do you want me to tell you?"

"A guy named Peterson."

"I don't know a guy named Peterson."

"That's the wrong answer."

"I knew Peterson in the Army."

"Wrong answer, Leo."

Leo was sweating. The sweat was everywhere. His face was shining with wetness.

"I thought we talked, you and me."

"We always talked."

"What deal did you have with Briggs?"

"I didn't, I swear to God I never made a deal with him."

"You and I always talked, Leo. I'm very disappointed in you. You working a separate deal now with the G?"

"G? I don't know no G."

"You know a G, all right. Named Peterson. He told me I was leaning on you so you musta told him."

"I don't know no G named Peterson or anything." He was screaming but the voice was quiet. The screaming was inside his head. "I swear on my mother's grave, I swear to God, Tommy."

"You didn't have a mother. Shit like you just happens," Tommy Gallagher said. The big pistol was right between them, right between Leo's eyes.

"What can I do to tell you? We was talking and you was telling me about this guy named Drover was looking into Dan Briggs and the next thing I know, I'm talking to Drover and then you're back at me about it because this Drover gives you my name. Then what was it, I was nervous. Bugs Rio wants to know why I'm talking to a cop and talking to this geek they seen me with and I tell him this guy is named Drover and he wants to ask me about Dan Briggs. That's all, Tommy. Nothing else. Jesus Christ, first that NCAA guy was on me last spring, that Cary Lucas, he wants to know about Dan Briggs and and I don't know nothin' about no Dan Briggs I tell him and then Danny kills himself. Fucker. He left me a dime's worth of markers, the prick."

"Leo, you're getting off the point. I want to know about a G."

"I swear, Tommy, I don't know about no G."

Gallagher waited for a long moment before letting down the hammer out of its cocked position. He put the piece away. He stared at Leo and lit a cigarette and let Leo shake in place.

"This goes down wrong, we all go down," Tommy Gallagher said.

"Nothing is going down wrong. I handle the change, I spread it around, nobody knows nothing about the games we play," Leo Myers said. "You and me."

"And Dan Briggs. And his partner. But now Dan Briggs is dead."

"So we can work it with one guy. All we gotta do is be cool for a while," Leo Myers said.

"You don't cross me, Leo. You cross me and you'll be deader than Dan Briggs is," Tommy Gallagher said. "Deader than winter."

Leo shivered again, a variation on the shakes. "What's this about?"

"This is about keeping quiet. Like the dagos say, *omertà*. Huh? You capeesh *omertà*, Shylock?"

"I'm a little guy, I don't wanna get squashed," Leo said. "You known me for ten years, Tommy."

"Guys change."

"I don't change."

Tommy Gallagher looked him up and down, the hard stare of the policeman who wants to put fear in a rat. It is a variation on the cold Outfit look; this one has a note of self-righteousness in it. Cops learn it along with how to use a baton to choke-hold a suspect and how to plant a throwaway on a dead body, and it isn't in the police academy.

Leo showed the fear in his rat eyes.

"Okay, Leo. I'm gonna drop you. You want me to drop you at Glasses or is that too early in the day for you?" Tommy Gallagher said. Leo was shivering, miserable, feeling down but alive. He was still alive.

"To tell you the truth, I need a drink," Leo Myers said.

TWENTY-SIX

Bugs Rio was sitting in the tavern called Glasses nursing a beer. The woman in the soap opera was talking very slowly and the man was opening her blouse very slowly. Soap opera people move like they're under water.

Leo Myers came in the back door and walked the whole length of the bar and sat down at a stool next to Bugs. The bartender named Curly came down the boards and said, "Coffee, Leo?"

"Give me a shooter," Leo said. "Beer back."

Curly set out the shot and beer and moved away. He didn't ever want to overhear a conversation between Bugs and Leo.

"You start early," Bugs said.

"I got a cold."

"Tea is better than that stuff."

"I know how to cure a cold," Leo said. He shuddered at the raw warmth of the whiskey. "You got news for me?"

"I got news for you. Steve March wants to find this guy Drover and tear him a new asshole. He went crazy yesterday. He beat the shit out of the broad that asked Drover to look into the Dan Briggs thing. It makes no sense but you can't force Steve to make sense sometimes. Anyway, Steve wants you to make a contact with our friend the zebra and shave on the Wisconsin-Northwestern game."

"Wisconsin-Northwestern? Who the hell bets that game?"

"He wants you to lay off twenty dimes this time," Bugs Rio said. Twenty thousand dollars.

"This is not a good time. Dan Briggs killing himself just weeks ago. I think we should keep our head down for a while, let the thing blow over," Leo said.

"Steve March is not asking for your suggestions," Bugs said. "Look, Leo, I'm a messenger. You got to make the contact. Steve is betting Northwestern. Put him down for twenty. The game goes off in five days. That's your time frame. Don't screw this up, Leo, you know how Steve can get."

Leo thought about it. Steve and Tommy, Tommy and Steve. Which guy could kill him deader? He felt like someone was closing a door and his hand was stuck in the jamb.

"Look, I'll level with you, Bugs, I always have." Two lies in one sentence was not a record for Leo. "I was rousted again by this dick, this Tommy Gallagher. The guy I tol' you come around to me twice asking about Dan Briggs. That makes me very nervous. I don' know nothin' about Dan Briggs but when police looies come around givin' a small-time book like me a hard time, they either want a shakedown or they want something serious. You gotta tell Steve this, tell him the sensible thing is to lay off."

Bugs thought about it. He stared at Leo's shaking hand reaching for the shooter. Leo was scared of something enough to tell Steve no.

"I can talk to Steve for you but I don't like it. Steve is in one of his upper moods. You know what I mean. He's bulletproof."

"I swear the guy was on dope."

"He doesn't need dope, he's his own high, jumping in that Buick all hours, driving around like a crazy man. He got into that thing on Rush Street a couple of years ago and beat the shit out of that lady cop, I mean, this is not a guy who thinks reasonable."

"The cops want to kill him for that. Instead, he's found not guilty of attempted manslaughter by that little guinea judge he bought," Leo said. "Sorry, Bugs."

"Yeah, don't use language like that if Steve was around."

"I said I was sorry. You gotta talk to Steve for me, you got to set him straight."

"I gotta, I gotta. You sound like a record. All right, I see it your way. I'll tell Steve about the cop. About him coming around again. Maybe Steve will be cool. Maybe he's got some reason he wants the money down on this game. But if I tell you that Steve wants the game shaved, you better get out your Gillette and start doing it because I would not want to be you if you cross him."

"I been getting threatened since I got up this morning."

"What's worse? A cop or Steve March?"

Leo stared at Bugs.

He didn't really have an answer.

TWENTY-SEVEN

FIONNA WOKE in her hospital bed, and Drover was sitting next to her bed. He had brought flowers and chocolate. A Whitman's Sampler.

"I haven't seen a Whitman's Sampler in years," she said. She smiled a little, but it hurt too much to smile a lot.

"I'm corny. I give away cookie jars as wedding presents. Full of Oreos. I like the simple things in life, good or bad. Hot dogs, day baseball, Oreo cookies, Skippy peanut butter. You know. It makes life uncomplicated when you give up trends."

"Why don't you kiss me?"

Simple enough. Drover bent over her and kissed her. Simple enough and very complicated. Drover felt a rush of guilt and it was like a high. What was he, a Boy Scout? You can never get over a crush. You see someone fifteen years later and you only remember the crush, the squeezing of your heart. Was he in love? Naw. Only a crush, but crushes hurt.

He sat down again and they looked at each other. Was she feeling it too, the sweet guilt of the thing? They had known each other when nice girls still didn't and touching breasts was illegal and Holy Mother Church thought all girls should wear girdles as another layer of protection.

"I'm sorry I asked you."

"What? To kiss you?"

"To get involved. I was dreaming about it. It really is sick, isn't it? What a tight little group we had down in North Fork. Me and Paul and Neil and Paul had Betsy and Betsy . . ."

"Hush."

She said, "How is Paul?"

"I don't know. I was in L.A. when I got your message."

"It was to stay away."

"Who did it?"

"I don't know."

"The cops know?"

"They're not telling me."

"What did he say exactly?"

"I don't want to repeat it."

"What was it, Fionna?"

"You know how angry it makes me. That someone could come into my apartment just like I didn't have locks on the doors and just beat me up like it didn't matter what I said or whether I screamed or not? I screamed and he hit me all the harder and he said, 'Sing out, cunt.' " She flushed. "What an ugly word."

"Nice word. Nice man."

"Go away, Jimmy. I don't know what this is but the police—"

"I talked to police. I talked to a guy with the NCAA this morning."

"What time is it?"

"Four in the afternoon."

"I keep sleeping and waking up. Hospitals make the days longer," Fionna said. She was pale, and her head was partially bandaged. Her eyes were blackened. She seemed shrunken, but it was just the weight of the bandages and her injuries. She was diminished and frail, a broken bird on the sidewalk. "He said, 'You told this Drover guy to stick his nose in. I'm gonna break your nose, you cunt, and you tell him I'm gonna break his prick off.' " She flushed again.

Drover stared. Then got up and walked to the end of the room and back. He was very angry and it made him very calm, something that went back to childhood. He could be made afraid, he could be bullied—there are always bigger guys on the block—but that was always an outside game to him. Slow to anger, even if he was taunted. When it came down to finally being angry, no one was bigger than Drover, not even King Kong.

"Somebody had it in for St. Mary's. Maybe your brother. Anonymous stuff and it's all mostly b.s. Except for one thing—your husband—"

"My soon-to-be ex-husband—"

He was going to say one thing and decided not to. "Neil O'Neill did some petty-ass cash when he recruited Albert Brown. It didn't amount to much but the NCAA guy Lucas is going to report it. So St. Mary's joins the real world and gets a slap on the wrist. Venial sin, Fionna. Why did your brother resign as coach? The NCAA doesn't have a thing on the rest of it."

"Did they tell hin that?" Her eyes turned bright. There was a bitter edge to her voice. "Did Father O wrap his arms around Paul when he resigned or was he just pushed over the ledge? Did Dave Zekman stand behind him? I read about it in the papers today. My brother was left alone out there, after all he gave St. Mary's all these years. Father O had no comment and Zekman was supposed to be out of town."

"Does Paul know you're hurt?"

"No. And he's not going to know." She was angry herself, it was putting color back in her wan cheeks. "He's got enough right now without that. Promise me."

"Promise."

They sat and stared at each other and Drover held her hand. She looked at her hand in his. She squeezed his hand suddenly. It was very schoolgirlish and he blushed and that was boyish and they were grown people who had lived through some of the things Janis Joplin sang about.

"Black Kelly was sweet. He brought the other flowers. He was here when I came back to the room from surgery. He was very sweet." Her voice softened. "I told his sister to tell you not to come back. Did Kelly tell you?"

"I go where I please."

"Oh, Jimmy. This man was a maniac. I mean, he was beating me up and talking to me at the same time. Like he was talking to himself."

"Well, we'll find him."

"You're not a policeman, leave it to them."

"I can't do it now. A couple of days ago, it was your problem and I was doing you a favor. Things changed."

"What changed?"

"Things."

She said, "I felt so odd when we . . . made love. I felt like I was twenty years old. I never made love to anyone until I married Neil. A virgin bride."

"It isn't that," he said.

"Isn't what?"

"Things changed but not because of that, Fionna. They changed because people don't have to accept a raw deal. A guy was killed, I know he was killed without knowing anything more. And the cops said it was a suicide because it was convenient to call it that. The NCAA was investigating a bunch of anonymous charges which is what the NCAA does. It really is the Spanish Inquisition, you know."

"Tell me," she said.

"College ball. Football or basketball. They just want to keep the lid on while they're scooping up the cash."

"Paul believes in it."

"I don't care if Paul believes the earth is flat, there's what he believes and what's true. You take a poor black kid like Albert Brown who has no chance in life at all, if he's lucky he can be night manager at a McDonald's when he's fifty. He suddenly develops this one thing that God gave him. He can play roundball. So he slogs his way through the shoe camps, shows his meat off to a bunch of predators in coach's clothing who stand around and figure out which of the Albert Browns on the court will be plucked up and given a college scholarship. College is the magic that's going to open all the doors for them, let them into white people's society as long as they shoot seven for ten at the free-throw line and mind their manners. They can't be paid, of course, that would be the same as turning whore. Forget that the college that buys the slaves makes millions from basketball shoe companies and television and radio and alumni donations. The old school ties, the alums can come down in their leased Caddys and cheer on the old team and maybe drop a few grand to refurbish the library. Which most of the slaves—the players—wouldn't even know how to spell, let alone know what's in it. Shit."

"Are you really that angry?"

"I'm really that angry. You shouldn't have called to me on the street the other night, Fionna, you're right. I have a nice uncompli-cated life. I live like a bum, sleep till noon, go to games, pretend I didn't used to be a writer. I've got a few girls I know and some I know even better and I am so damned footloose that no one can pin me down."

"What changed?"

"Honey, I don't like to be pushed around. Maybe it was old home week. I didn't want old home week."

"Me?"

"It's all I can do to stop crawling into that bed with you. That's the good part, Fionna. I don't know why it happened but I'm glad it did. What changed was listening to Paul the other morning talk about honor and truth and justice. It's knowing that anyone who believes in that shit is going to fall into the mire. What do you think Father O wants? He wants winners because winners bring money."

"Paul brought him a winner—"

"Neil brought him a winner. Bought is the better word. A few hundred here and a few hundred there and Neil played the game because he really, basically, underneath it all, didn't give a shit. It was a racket and he knew it."

"He helped Paul—"

"It didn't cost him a nickel. He was getting back at this Dave Zekman and getting back at you."

She blinked then. Her eyes were wet.

"He called you and Paul the Bobbsey Twins. I might have popped him. Except it was true."

There. She withdrew her hand and it hurt him. He was staring at her and she was on the verge of real tears, the kind that roll down your cheeks.

"Honey."

Fionna got a stubborn look then.

"Fionna, I don't want memories. I don't visit my mother's grave because I see her every night. I don't want to go to class reunions and see what we all turned into. I don't want dreams, real or broken. I just want to live today and tomorrow. You lived in a dream all those years. With Paul and Neil. For Christ's sake, you still were in North Fork. You saw Father O and you said, 'Father O,' just like you were in the third row in theology class."

"You done? I mean, making fun of me? Of Paul? I guess we didn't get as sophisticated as you'd want. Hicks in Indiana. As Neil wanted. Is that it? Neil wanted more?"

"I don't know what Neil wanted when he had you. If I had had you, I would have retired all my wants," Drover said.

Silence. The humming kind of hospital silence that can be broken at any moment by an intrusive nurse pushing a tray of lukewarm hospital mush.

"I don't understand you," she finally said. Soft and wondering. Her mouth was open. He remembered that. He had once studied her mouth during a semester in poly sci. When she was trying to understand something—the course had been good enough to be difficult—her mouth would halfway open and her tongue would worry her teeth and the unconscious habit fascinated him more than anything on earth.

"I talk too much sometimes. When I get mad. It blows off a little steam."

"Who are you mad at?"

"The man who beat you up. But I'll get him, I don't have any doubts about that. I just have to figure out what to do with him when I get him."

"Don't, Jimmy." Hand again. "I really mean it. When he was hitting me and I was screaming at him, trying to hit him back, I was just so damned scared. I thought he was going to rape me and then I thought, no, he doesn't want to rape me, he just wants to kill me. And I thought I was going to die."

"You're not going to die. You're safe, Fionna."

"But if you stay here, he'll come for you."

"Exactly. He'll fall into my trap."

"What trap?"

Drover grinned. "Well, I haven't figured that part out yet. Just take it on faith. It's like writing an article. I usually start at the beginning and get to the middle and wonder where the hell I go from here. But I always finish the piece, right on deadline. So believe."

"Like believing the earth is flat."

Drover kept smiling then.

"Yeah. Exactly like that."

TWENTY-EIGHT

D<small>ROVER OPENED</small> the door to his room in the Drake Hotel and saw the message light flickering. He closed the door and took off his well-traveled clothes and went to the shower. After ten minutes of soaping and running water down his skin, Drover felt human enough to face the real world, the one he had preached about when Fionna was too weak to resist. Why had he done it? Because nothing made him angrier than people who fooled themselves. Maybe he was more like Neil O'Neill than he realized. The Bobbsey Twins. Yeah, Neil had got that right. It was cruel and unfair but it was right on the money. What kind of a dim bulb surrenders to his enemies before they lob a Scud missile at him? He had wanted to shake Fionna and then he had wanted her to run away with him to Santa Cruz and spend the rest of her life on the beach and in his arms. Stupid schoolboy crush. He had prettier girls but you can't get over remembering your youth and how you could live for days on pure, unbridled, unrequited lust.

Messages.

"A message from Mr. Kelly."

"A second message from Mr. Kelly. That came in today."

"A message from a Mr. Peterson and a telephone number."

"A message from a Mr. Smith."

"What message?"

"Mr. Smith says Fionna got off easy."

"Mr. Smith leave a telephone number?"

"That was the entire message, sir."

"Okay. Anything else?"

"Mr. Carmody." She gave the number but Drover already knew it.

The real world is contained in messages left with an operator or answering machine. Everything is a callback. Some people use telephones like instruments of torture, to inflict pain on others. And some people, like Drover, cringe when a telephone rings. It is always bad news because bad news can't wait for the post office.

"Kelly? How can you spend all day and night in a saloon and not get drunk?"

"I pace myself," Kelly said. "Besides, I only order a child's portion. Noonan came up with a recipe for jambalaya—"

"Jambalaya doesn't need a recipe. What's up?"

"Steve March."

"Who's he?

"A jambrone. He likes to beat up women. He beat up a woman cop a couple of years ago and walked. Everyone says he bought the judge."

"How did you get the name?"

"I asked my cousin in the department, Barney."

"Is there anyone in Chicago you're not related to?"

"Just you. And we're not sure of you," Kelly said. "The cops want Fionna to eyeball him. They're looking for him now. They'll find him."

"And what will that mean?"

"It means he'll get eyeballed and charged and he'll be back on the street all within a few hours. It's criminal justice in action," Kelly said.

"I want better than that."

"The cops would like better than that. He's connected."

"Connected. You sure?"

"Yeah, I'm sure. I mean, he doesn't carry a card that says he's a member in good standing with the Outfit, but Barney says he's connected."

"When did the cops know it was him?"

"Right away."

"It's a day later."

"There was a debate going on, I guess. I'm not privy to this, but Barney, well, Barney says that there was some question about how to take Steve March in. There was a majority that wanted him to resist arrest but cooler heads prevailed."

"That's Barney's theory. What I want to know is why is it a day later?"

"I don't know. Barney doesn't know."

"I begin to think I know," Drover said. He was naked, his skin was shower-warm, and he was staring at the phone while he was seeing something else play in his mind. It was like connect-the-dots.

"You know what?"

"I know what. Exactly. Anything else?"

"You gonna be safe in your hotel room?"

"Snug as a bug. You want to eat?"

"Sure. I'll cruise over to the Golden Ox and reserve a table. How about seven?"

"Sure. Later." They broke the connection.

The phone rang a long time and then a voice said, "Hello?"

"Me, Mr. Peterson."

"Who's me?"

"Your favorite sportswriter from California."

"You got my message."

"No. I just thought I'd call you up for a date. Or are you washing your hair tonight?"

"Gallagher made a mistake when he didn't book you."

"Well, mistakes happen. Like the mistake you made pulling your rank on Gallagher. And on me. And on the NCAA. Whatever you're doing, you are obstructing a helluva lot of justice in getting it done."

"I want to talk to you."

"I bet. Covering up a murder is the kind of thing that gives the FBI a bad reputation. You're supposed to be the good guys."

"I can be at your hotel in fifteen minutes. Maybe twenty, twenty-five with the rush hour."

"Use your G-man siren. But don't hurry. I'll meet you at seven for dinner. The Golden Ox. You know it?"

"I know it. I'm not hungry."

"But I am."

Drover broke the connection this time. Then he phoned again the familiar old number.

"Yeah?" Not "hi" or "hello" or anything that might indicate charm. Charm was what people used to conceal their weakness.

"Yeah yourself," Drover said.

"I wanna talk to you, kid," Carmody said.

"Did you talk to your protégé?"

"I talked to him."

"What'd he say?"

"I wanna talk to you."

Drover sighed. A certain generation and a certain class of men—hardly ever women—consider the telephone to be a temporary device used by people on crutches to get around. When you want to talk to someone, you talked to him face-to-face.

"All right, Captain. I'm going over to the Golden Ox to eat at seven. With my friend Kelly. Come along and I'll buy supper."

"I know the Ox, was always in a bad neighborhood."

"So what? You scared?"

Silence.

"What's this guy Kelly to our business?"

"What I know, Kelly knows."

"Is that a fact?"

"No, I just made it up. Captain, you coming or not?"

"You carrying?"

"I beg your pardon."

"Carrying," Carmody said.

"I don't have a gun if that's what you mean."

"Can you get one?"

"No. I don't want one."

"Then watch yourself, kid."

"Watch myself?"

"See you at seven. I'll be heavy. You tell your fireman friend he might want to be heavy."

Click.

Drover blinked, thinking it out. So who didn't call him?

Tommy Gallagher.

Tommy didn't want to talk to him.

Maybe he didn't have anything more to say.

Drover sighed and got up and started to rummage through his bag for clean clothes.

TWENTY-NINE

FIONNA GOT Paul on the phone around five. He said "h'lo" in the sullen way he had adopted in his fifteenth year, feeling hormones and feeling alienated. He was past hormonal development now. He said he was home, feeling miserable. Betsy was shopping with the kids as though nothing had happened except that Paul was hanging around the house today instead of being at the gym. Paul didn't tell Fionna this until she asked about Betsy. For the first time in his life, he felt alone. He was sure he had never felt alone before. Home life had merged into school days and one had become part of the other and he had always known where he stood with people. There was a hierarchy to the universe he had inhabited until last night, until the press conference where nobody showed up. And now this. He was naked and nobody had called him all day except for news reporters who wanted interviews. And Neil O'Neill who, after commiserating, wanted an interview.

"I talked to Jimmy Drover," she said finally.

"Don't bring up his name."

"He talked to the man in the NCAA," Fionna said. "The man told him there was one small thing at St. Mary's and it wasn't you, it didn't involve you, it involved some kind of recruiting violation with Neil recruiting Albert Brown."

Despite himself, he was listening.

"Paul? Why did you quit the team?"

Silence. It was very cold in northern Indiana, and the snow on the broken fields was arranged in drifts. Trees were bare, sketches against the darkening sky. Every afternoon, evening crept in earlier and earlier. Betsy was buying Christmas presents and hiding them in the closet upstairs. Little Paul would get a Nintendo game this year. Somehow, he was removed from all this now, just barely alive except for this disembodied voice of his sister.

"Paul? Are you there?"

"I don't know," Paul said.

"Paul. Snap out of it. Where's Betsy?"

"She went Christmas shopping, where else? I just quit my job and she went Christmas shopping. She doesn't believe anything really happened. Father O'Brien hasn't called me all day. Man I've known for almost fifteen years. Trusted."

"Paul, stop it. Listen to me."

What was that tone in her voice? What did she think was happening to him? He wasn't going to do anything crazy. He wasn't going to kill himself. That would be a mortal sin, absolutely unforgivable because there would be no breath of life in his body when he wanted forgiveness. God would judge him and send him to hell. A real hell.

Paul shivered even though the house was as warm as a fireplace. He was wandering across the farm fields, snow up to his ass, trying to take another step and then another, soaked through with wet cold . . .

"Paul. I'd slap your face if I was there. Why did you quit?"

"Fi, I had to quit."

"Why?"

"I can't tell you."

"You can tell me anything. You always have."

It was true. His sister was himself. They were beautiful children, everyone had said that. They played together. She was popular, he was less popular, but he made the team, he was really beautiful on a basketball court, the roundball arcing so beneath the girder trestles of the gym, swishing home through the basket, the net making a whisper against the skin of the ball . . .

"Paul, I want you to tell me. Jimmy is in danger, he did this for you—"

"I told you, I told you the other day, don't do anything for me. I told you that. I told them. I told Father O and Dave Zekman. They told the NCAA. I didn't do anything wrong, Fi, I tried to tell them that and they just looked at me. You know what I mean?"

He was sobbing.

"Paul, Paul, Paul honey, listen to me, honey, listen to Fi. Listen to me."

After a while, the sobs stopped. His eyes were wet and they burned with salty tears.

"Paul, why did you resign? Now, you can tell Fi, I won't tell anyone."

"You have to promise."

"I promise."

Silence.

"Paul?"

"I talked to Albert Brown when the NCAA announced its investigation. Yesterday afternoon. We really talked this time. Sometimes, he didn't even look at me. Didn't look at me."

"Paul—"

"It was during practice and we went into my office. He's so scared. He knows he did something wrong and I could feel it, I could feel he wanted to tell me. We said a prayer together and he started to cry. He said his mama was so good, his mama wouldn't do anything wrong, she didn't know, Albert didn't think it was wrong. I said what was wrong and he told me. He told me."

"He told you."

"He told me about the money."

"What money?"

Silence.

"He said his mama made three dollars an hour in the laundry cleaning up. Three dollars an hour. He knew how much everything cost. The rent cost so much and his auntie made five dollars an hour cleaning people's houses, white, rich people, and it took her an hour and a half on the bus each way to get to where the rich people lived. There was his aunt, his mama, his sister who was still in school, there was Albert who should have a job . . . Didn't I know all this? I knew this and I told Albert he could have a scholarship to St. Mary's College and it wasn't enough for him, a scholarship wasn't going to get his mama out of working herself down to nothing for three dollars an hour."

Silence. No sobs but the silence was enough crying.

"Neil went down after I did. To North Carolina. I told him everything, I told Neil there was no way Albert was going to come to St. Mary's. Then, like a miracle, Albert was here. I knew then it had to be something. Albert could have gone to some place where there's money to be made."

"It was a small violation, Paul, it was Neil's violation anyway, not yours. It was small change. Petty cash, Drover said."

"It was five thousand dollars," Paul said. He was cold again, not crying, just laying out numbers the way Albert Brown laid out numbers in his office. Albert knew what apples cost in winter and knew what the price of his uniform was in the Catholic high school he had attended. Five thousand dollars.

"Five thousand dollars? He told you that Neil gave him five thousand dollars?"

"No. He said it was a couple of hundred. And then a couple of hundred. And another couple of hundred. Where was Neil getting money from?"

"Where was he?"

"I told Albert not to worry and just be the best player he could be. I told him I'd say a prayer for him and he left me alone and I thought about it. Where was the money coming from over a year, hundreds of dollars? Was Neil paying out of his own pocket?"

"Neil was buying Albert."

"Isn't that what we do, Fi? In the end? We're buying kids who don't know their own worth," Paul said.

"Paul, you didn't know—"

"But I had to know because I knew that Albert wasn't going to go to St. Mary's and then he was suddenly here and Neil was smiling like the Cheshire cat and I just kept silent, hoping it had just been a miracle. Neil's silver tongue had done it. Or Albert wanted to be a brain surgeon when he graduated. I had to know. Neil knew and he would smile at me when we watched Albert in practice. Neil knew what he was doing. He was buying a team."

"Someone had to know."

Silence. And then Paul spoke carefully, carefully as an old man walking with a cane on an icy street.

"It was about five, I think, I was in shock, I went down to Dave Zekman's office and I started to tell him. He held up his hand. He told me to not tell him anything, to let the NCAA prove its case."

"Why would you tell Dave Zekman? He's not your friend."

"I said I couldn't do things like that, that he was the A.D. and I had a duty to tell him things and I started to tell him and he said, 'Paul, why don't you give your confessional urge a rest. Just rest it.' Like that. And it dawned on me. Remember that horrible story? I think it was in philosophy class. About Thomas Aquinas at the end of his days suddenly, one day, Saint Thomas said he had been wrong. Wrong. "Summa Theologica," everything he had written, the careful philosophy and theology, suddenly Saint Thomas went berserk and died less than a month later. What had been wrong? The philosophical method? Or the conclusion he had reached?

"I don't know what you're talking about."

"God. Does He exist?"

"Paul, Paul, I think you should—"

"Don't you see, Fi?" Paul saw it. Why didn't this voice on the telephone see it?

"What? What are you talking about, Paul?"

"Dave Zekman. He knew, Fionna. He knew. He knew and Neil knew and Albert knew and probably Father O knew and the only jerk was me. I was the true believer. I was the only one who didn't know."

THIRTY

THE GOLDEN OX survived its slum surroundings. Now the triangle where Clybourn Street runs a slant pattern into North Avenue was gentrified to an excruciating degree, and the old German restaurant was going to survive that as well. The bar was beer hall bright, and florid faces fed on Wiener schnitzel and flagons of beer. Just the kind of joint for a cheerful sit-down with a retired Irish cop who used to kill gangsters, an FBI man who was covering up a homicide, and a gentle Irish saloonkeeper transplanted to California who used to be in the business of fighting holocausts and rescuing children from the flames.

That's what Drover thought when he entered the room, sat down with Kelly at the bar, and waited. "We have guests coming and I want a witness," Drover said.

"I like it when you involve me. You never give away too much and that makes it interesting for me," Kelly said. He waved an empty glass at the barman. "A child's portion," he said, yet again.

"Red Label, rocks, soda back," Drover said.

"This is serious. I thought Red Label was your Sunday drink."

"At nineteen bucks a bottle, it's become a religious exercise. But today is special. I talked to Fionna."

"Did you give her a kiss for me?"

"I gave her a kiss for me," Drover said.

"Ah," Kelly said. "The ways of wayward youth. Are you smitten again? Last time it was Lori Gibbons, the flight attendant who will become a microbe hunter in her next life."

"Lori and I are friends. Even more than friends. But Lori is on the golden shuttle now to Japan and serves wine and food to the more interesting class. First class. Big-money people. I think she thinks of me as a small pleasure, like eating a box of chocolates. She can do it once in a while but not all the time if she wants to keep her figure."

"Drover as a bonbon. I never thought of that metaphor or simile or whatever it was, but it fits. You have a reason you invited other people?"

"I always have a reason. It just doesn't occur to me right now."

Carmody and Peterson came through the door almost at the same time. There were snowflakes melting on their shoulders.

"God, it's starting to snow again," Kelly said.

Carmody and Peterson went straight up to Drover at the bar and then realized each other's presence. Drover introduced them and introduced Kelly. Reluctantly, the cop and the G-man followed Drover and Kelly to the dining room. The waitress took drink orders and went away. The room was out of kitsch central, a duster's nightmare of small, insignificant, and heroically silly objects perched on mantels.

"We can talk or we can eat first," Drover said.

Peterson said, "What kind of a game is this?"

"Endgame," Drover said.

"Is that right?"

"Captain, this here FBI is obstructing justice. Covering up a murder. As in murder."

"Is that right?"

Carmody, to his credit, barely glanced at Peterson. He kept his eyes on Drover. Peterson might have been someone's kid, tagging along at the dinner table where he should observe the decorum of being seen and not heard.

"Is that right?" Peterson repeated Carmody's question in a slightly more querulous tone.

"That's right. Dan Briggs was murdered. The NCAA was told that whatever it was that Briggs was doing was not the business of the NCAA. Which is bullshit. So the NCAA backs off because, after all, you are the G and everyone backs off the G. Right to Tommy Gallagher who started making the same noises with a two-bit bookie named Leo Myers and was told to back off again, by the same obstructionist G-man. You. You know how long it took me to see it? Right to this afternoon, seeing Fionna Givens in the hospital. Right to finding out that a guy named Steve March might or might not be picked up for assault and battery. You hear that name, Peterson?"

Carmody decided to inspect Peterson again, a bit more closely.

Peterson had the federal veneer—marble and the Great Seal burned into wood—but it just might be showing worn spots.

"I don't know what you're talking about."

Even Kelly, who had supplied the information, didn't know what Drover was talking about.

"The cops don't need a map to find this Steve March, do they?"

"He's a dago punk who bought a judge a couple of years ago after he beat up a woman. A policewoman he beat up." Carmody growled. "He lives out in Elmwood Park."

"But he's not being brought in because of Peterson. The well-known obstructionist."

"You wanna fuck with me, Drover?" Peterson was dipping into the tiresome federalese employed by Justice Department officials after seeing too many cop movies. Life imitates art because cops want to sound more like cops sometimes. Criminals expect it.

"Cut it out, Peterson," Drover said.

The waitress brought drinks. She announced the specials to four tight-lipped men who were staring at each other. She felt she wasn't wanted and traipsed away.

"You're doing an investigation. Involving a bookie named Myers and his ultimate boss, Steve March, the king of the street collectors.

I don't know who's your source but it's someone in that food chain and you don't give a rat's ass about the murder of a referee because everything is linked, isn't it? How long do we have to wait for the RICO indictments? A year more. Two years. You asshole. Murder is murder."

"Is that right?"

"Captain, tell the man murder is murder."

"You like talking, you keep talking," Carmody said. The growl in his voice was a shade deeper.

"And where is my good friend, the guy you recommended to me, Mr. Stand-up? You find him today like I asked you?"

"I talked to him," Carmody said.

"Who?" said Peterson.

"In a minute. I hope you're paying attention, Black. There'll be a written exam, multiple choice."

"I hate multiple choice. All the answers look right to me," Black Kelly said. His big hands had moved to the top of the table, near the edge. He was watching the cop and the G-man. His thumbs were hooked under the table edge, just in case this turned out to be the end of a poker game in a John Wayne Western.

"You'll get an A. Every choice is right. What did Mr. Stand-up say?"

Carmody said nothing for a moment. "He said you were gonna get yourself killed over nothing. He said it would be a mistake but you'd still be dead. I said what was he talking about? He said the Outfit was putting you on its list. He said that Leo Myers was Outfit and there was some kind of a racket going on and whatever it was, you were going to be whacked."

"I'm shivering in my boots," Drover said. In fact, he wasn't feeling as good as he talked.

"Who told you that?" Peterson said.

Drover turned back to him. "Come on, give it a try. Three guesses. It wasn't Groucho Marx. It wasn't Margaret Dumont."

Peterson glared. "You think this is a joke?"

"Yeah, I do. Hilarious in fact. Except I'm not playing. You're going to wrap up this investigation or it's going front-page. I always wanted to say something like that. It's every newspaperman's dream.'

"You couldn't buy your way on to a paper."

"Newspapers are run by two classes of people. The upper class is editorial and speaks of journalism with a capital J. The lower class is newspapermen. They don't give a shit. They run with it, as we used to say. They get a story and make it sing. And the upper class lets the lower class think the papers belong to them because they work cheap and it keeps up their enthusiasm. Sort of the way Mrs. Graham thinks she had something to do with Woodward and Bernstein. Or vice versa."

"What are you going to tell the papers, smart guy?"

"Good. You like that, Black? 'Smart guy.' Next thing he'll be calling me a wise apple. Boo-boop-de-do. That's early federal talk, back when G-men tried to dress like Jimmy Cagney. 'Smart guy.' Lovely."

"I don't really enjoy being your punching bag," Peterson said.

"What are you going to do? Get the IRS to audit me more than once a year? You already do that. Since my name came up, I'll bet you've scoured the federal building to build a record on me. What are you going to do to me, G-man? Deprive me of my livelihood? People like you already did that once in L.A. You going to say I hang out with a lower class of people? I admit it. They're more interesting than people you meet at a Winnetka dinner party. I talk to anyone. I even talk to federal agents who want to put me under false arrest. I saved your ass on that one, Peterson. Come to think of it, though, it wasn't me. It was my buddy. Captain Carmody's buddy. Everybody's buddy of the year. Lieutenant Tommy Gallagher."

Peterson very nearly didn't give it away. Just a slight tic to the left eyelid.

"What about him?"

"He's part of your investigation, isn't he?"

Carmody said, "You're full of shit, kid."

"No, you are. Captain, I admire the hell out of you because you did it the old-fashioned way. In your day. You and your friends would go out and bump off the wise guys because there was no way to get them into prison by legitimate means. You probably did society many favors we can't thank you for and you don't want us to mention. Having made that gracious introduction, we go to the first act: Tommy Gallagher is kinky. Isn't he, Peterson? He told you the Mob is after me. It isn't the Mob, Captain."

"Who is it?"

"Multiple choice. What profession, besides the criminal calling, carries guns? A. Firemen. B. Postal workers. C. Cops."

Drover looked at Peterson.

"What do you say?"

"I don't know what you're talking about."

"Who's wired? You got who wired exactly?"

"What wire?" Carmody said.

Drover said, "You guys don't want to play. Tommy Gallagher is a kink. It has to do with Leo Myers. I think it had to do with Dan Briggs. Briggs knew Myers. Briggs was killed. Next thing I know, Fionna Givens asked me to look into it. I go to Captain and he sends me to Gallagher. Fine. Gallagher shows me a police report calling Briggs's death a suicide. Next thing I know, he's slapping Leo Myers around, demanding to know who killed Dan Briggs. That's where you came in, Peterson. You called him off. But how the hell does that lead to Steve March's knocking down Fionna's door and warning me to back off and beating up Fionna? I mean, who told Steve about Fionna, down to her name and address? I don't know any Steve. I don't bring up Fionna's name to a piece of shit like Leo Myers when I talked to him. So, who puts a bug up Steve? And why isn't Steve in the clink, what you G-men like to call the slammer in your macho way? Because, you justice-obstructing asshole, you told the cop command to back down. Because you have a federal investigation ongoing. I'll bet Tommy Gallagher's name came up on one of your wires. And who is the wire anyway? Peterson, Tommy Gallagher rattled off Fionna's name to you and you gave it to your snitch in the investigation and your snitch gave it to Steve March." He stopped suddenly. "Or Gallagher gave out her name. Shit!"

Peterson just stared at him for a long moment. His drink was untouched and it was making a water spot spread on the tablecloth. Then he got up slowly, staring at Drover, letting his hatred seep into Drover's skin. "You screw this up, you'll be the sorriest man who was ever born."

"Yeah. But you'll have a few bad mornings too. What's it going to be, Peterson?"

A very long silence played out against the Muzak.

"I've got to make some calls," the agent said.

"What time should I expect this to be finished?"

"I didn't promise anything."

"Then I will. Four tomorrow afternoon. That gives you about twenty hours. If you don't use the post office, you can make it, I know you can. Use the phone and the fax machine."

"I didn't promise anything."

"That's all right. I'll cover your drink. Is it a legitimate expense? Can I claim it? Will you back it up? 'Money spent entertaining a federal agent.'"

"I wasn't entertained," Peterson said.

"Neither was I. Neither was Fionna Givens."

Very slowly, Peterson turned his back on the table and walked out of the room.

They watched him go in silence. There was no release of tension at the table. The focus shifted to the big retired police captain with the gut and the bulge of a gun under his coat.

Black Kelly said, "How do you figure things like that out?"

"You did it. You got me Myers. I got Myers because I was interested in Dan Briggs. Gallagher was going to blow me off from the first about Briggs and once a cop makes up his mind, you can't change it. The suicide was a suicide. But then I start on him, telling him about Fionna. My mistake. It cost Fionna and that makes me mad because I did it to her. Trusting your protégé."

"Tommy Gallagher is as good a cop as I know," Carmody said.

"Sure, and he sells you that booga-booga about the Outfit being after me so that when he whacks me later, you'll back him up. After all, I'm no good, Cap, isn't that right? Hanging out with known figures, getting indicted by a two-bit D.A. in L.A.? Right? I was the son you almost had. Thank God you could transfer your allegiance to someone decent like Tommy Gallagher."

Carmody sat there a long time, letting it get under his skin, even letting the sarcasm fill his chest and expand until it was in his bowels. He kept staring at Drover like a dead man. Drover didn't look away and Kelly thought if he put his hand between them, the skin would burn right off the bone.

"I seen Peterson take a walk," Carmody said at last.

"We all saw it."

"What do you think Tommy Gallagher was doing in all this?"

"I don't know, Captain. But he drives a thirty-five-thousand-dollar car and dresses nice. Do you know where he lives?"

"Some place downtown, he rents an apartment in . . ."

"Fuck rent. He owns a condominium on Chestnut Street, off Michigan Avenue. I don't know what it cost him but I'll bet it's more than the superintendent could afford. Tommy is a high liver in a quiet way and Peterson had to notice that as much as I did. After all, he's the federal agent, not me. I spent an hour and half with a roll of quarters on phone calls and I can do a thumbnail of Tommy Gallagher that makes him kinkier than leather in July. What could Peterson do with a little effort? Or an old harness bull like you, Captain?"

Carmody was shaking his head from side to side. Slowly and sadly.

"Jesus, kid. Tommy Gallagher. I swear to God . . ."

"I know."

"Jesus Christ."

By some incredible act of will, the old man did not even let his eyes get wet. He got up from the table and they both saw the bulge of the pistol in his belt. He was a big man and it was a big gun. He had shot it out in the wild days of the 1950s, working the West Side where bodies hung in meat lockers and the Outfit ran everything but the trolley barns. But all that bulk was now a shell, framed around a past that had no relevance.

"I'm sorry, kid."

Drover understood. Now he could look away. "I know, Captain."

"Sorry."

"I know, Captain. I'm sorry too."

"And to the girl. I never would have hurt the hair on a woman's head, I don't care who."

"I know, Captain."

"Tommy in with the guineas."

"I don't know that. I just know about Myers."

"The same thing. Jews, Irish, Polacks, Italians, Sicilians, they're all the same thing when they're in with the vowels."

It didn't make sense but Drover let it go. He understood the vacant look in Carmody's eyes. No steel there at all. The hearths were banked and the workers had gone home.

He walked out of the place and only stumbled once against an empty chair. They sat there and the waitress came back.

"You boys eating?" she said. She must have been all of fifty.

Drover looked at his empty glass.

"Red Label, rocks," he said.

They had another round.

THIRTY-ONE

"SHE DISCHARGED herself two hours ago," the nurse said. She wasn't happy about it and wasn't happy about these two men coming in at 8:00 P.M. to see a female patient when they both, obviously, had been drinking.

"She could do that?"

"This isn't a prison," the nurse said. "Who are you?"

"Friends."

Drover and Kelly went to the pay telephone bank on one wall of the lobby near the gift shop. Drover punched in the numbers of her home phone. It rang and rang and rang. Then he thought to call the Drake Hotel and pick up his messages.

"Yes, Mr. Drover, there's a message. 'Fionna called and said something has happened to Paul.' That's the message."

"All right," Drover said. He looked at Kelly. "Something about Paul. She's gone to St. Mary's."

"On a night like this. There'll be a foot of snow in Indiana. I had a summer place once in Grand Beach over on the Michigan side and I wanted to use it year-round but I could never drive to Michigan in the winter months. So I gave it up."

"Wonderful anecdote. We'll fly."

"That's my style exactly."

The woman for the feeder line to North Fork was very nice.

"I'm sure we'd have room but not tonight. No flying out tonight. Not until it stops snowing," she explained on the phone. "O'Hare is slow but possible, but North Fork Regional is shut down."

Drover replaced the receiver and looked at Black Kelly. Kelly said, "At least I got a heavy Cadillac rental. Grinds down the snow. What happens if we get stuck?"

"What happens if Fionna gets stuck?"

"Maybe she isn't there."

"She's there."

"All right. Why don't you call her? I like dealing with you West Side types, you're all afraid of telephones, even when you're honest."

They called directory assistance and were told that the telephone number for Paul Givens was unlisted. Then Drover tried Father O's number.

A whispery voice answered and said that Father O'Brien was out for the evening and was there any message.

"Is it snowing hard at St. Mary's?"

"Just terrible," the whisperer said.

"Great," Drover said. "I'll bring my skis."

He hung up the phone.

Kelly shrugged. "I'll drive."

"You're the designated. I'm sort of pooped."

"Do you think we could take along a bottle of brandy in case we get stuck? I mean, for the medicinal value of it?"

"Sure. But I doubt the hospital gift shop has any."

Kelly stopped at an all-night Walgreen's and picked up a bottle of Christian Brothers finest and a pound of M&M's.

"Candy and brandy," Drover said. "I didn't know about your sweet tooth."

"Back in sixty-seven when we had the big snow, my brother-in-law was stuck two days on I-80 in Nebraska and he said he lived on cold coffee and that the candy kept him warm. Sugar is fuel, Drover, didn't you learn anything in biology?"

"Girls are different from boys."

They were on the Skyway heading south and east out of Chicago twenty minutes later. The Skyway is a big, long bridge that shoots up over the neighborhood of South Chicago and reduces church spires to spikes down there. The Skyway was nearly empty of traffic as it usually is, but it was slick where the snow had been plowed and packed down. The flakes were whiting out the landscape. The big flakes slammed into the glare of the headlamps and reflected the light back to the driver, making him half-blind when it came to watching the road and the direction of the car. Kelly was behind the wheel and tooled the Cadillac like he had made all the payments on it. "Dashing through the snow, in a one-horse open sleigh," he began to sing.

Drover stared out the window. Something had happened to Paul.

"Never do a favor for an old flame," Drover said.

Kelly didn't look at him. His eyes were on the road, trying to see into the darkness between the giant flakes rushing the windshield. "Is there a note of self-pity in your voice, lad? Drover should be made of sterner stuff."

"Yeah, you're right. But I got her involved more than she got me involved, right down to getting beat up by a psycho named Steve March whom the cops don't want to do anything about."

"You don't know cops then. The cops would like to kick the hell out of him, I'll bet. But when the federal agents put a thing down, it's done," Kelly said. "Very frustrating life. That's why you don't ever want to drink with policemen. Life is bad enough drinking with ordinary drunks but policemen have guns when they get drunk."

"Wise words," Drover said.

The car skidded and plowed its way across the state line and Drover nodded at the Cline Avenue exit in Gary. "Get off here or we'll get stuck up ahead, they've probably closed down the toll road by now."

It took nearly three hours this way, but they made it. It was just short of midnight and North Fork was pretty and deserted except for orange-painted plow trucks fighting the snow to a standstill along the main streets.

Kelly was munching from the M&M's bag, cruising the orange-lit streets, smiling a little. "So this is where you went to college. Your formative years spent in a hick town in Indiana. It explains a lot, Drover."

"Explains what?

"Things. Puzzling aspects of your personality I've noticed. Very provincial, very chauvinistic, very . . . well, unsophisticated."

Drover grunted and settled back in his seat and watched the cityscape unfold. He gave directions laconically. Left here, right there. They crossed the town to the darker, gentler depths of the campus. They spotted a campus police car parked under an elm near the chapel and pulled up. Kelly powered down his window and the cop did the same.

"We're looking for Paul Givens's house," Kelly said.

"Why?"

"My name is Knobby Walsh," Kelly said. "NCAA."

"You guys. The reason the coach tried to kill himself."

Drover leaned across Knobby Walsh's bulk. "What are you talking about?"

"He's in Memorial Hospital. He swallowed a bottle of Valium. They pumped him out, but it was you guys. St. Mary's isn't UNLV, you want to find recruiting violations, go someplace else, leave a decent school alone." The campus cop was full of cold contempt and he was spitting it out across to Kelly. Kelly blinked at him with mild, blue eyes, the way a polite foreigner will wait until the American has blustered to the end of his speech and then inform him he doesn't understand a word of English.

"We came to see his sister. Fionna O'Neill."

"Coach O'Neill's wife? I don't know anything about her."

Kelly powered up the window and they crunched tires across virgin snow back to the turnoff leading to town.

"I don't think we're going to get admitted to a hospital at midnight," Kelly said.

"Maybe she's there."

But she wasn't. She had been there but she wasn't there. Everyone had gone home. The hospital was small, sterile, and depressing, exactly the way hospitals are supposed to be.

The desk clerk had gone to bed at the Motel 6 but he came out in pajamas and a bathrobe to register two more customers. Drover asked his question.

"Yes, she's registered. You want me to ring her?"

"Yes, please."

It couldn't happen in a big city but small towns still have a measure of trust and every stranger isn't out to get you. The old man rang Fionna's room and she answered on the fourth ring.

"Mr. Drover and Mr. Kelly just registered and asked me to ring you, Miss Givens," the old man said.

He nodded to the phone, replaced it, and nodded to the two men. "She said knock on her door." He wasn't trying to be suspicious now, it wasn't neighborly, but it was coming out anyway. For some absurd reason, Drover felt he had to justify himself. Maybe it was the leftover guilt working on him.

"I'm her brother-in-law," Drover said. "We heard about Paul."

"Everyone's heard about Paul's trying to kill himself," the old man said.

"I'd appreciate knowing her room number so I don't have to knock on every door," Drover said.

"Oh. Yes. I suppose she told me to send you along." He still didn't like it. "Room two-oh-six. And you men are in two-sixty-five, go around back and there's an entrance."

"Thanks."

"Pleasure," the old man said, not meaning a word of it.

THIRTY-TWO

T HE SNOWY night was full of games.

DePaul was stuck in South Bend and they decided to make the best of it by beating up the Fighting Irish in the creaky old gym Notre Dame uses at home. The Notre Dame crowd is a big part of any home game, but DePaul took them out of the game by the third quarter and the silence hung in the place like an accusation. The game was tel-evised coast to coast and between dribbles, lay-ups, post patterns set out, and baseline jumpers, there were Hondas, Toyotas, Coca-Colas, Reeboks, a sequel to *Terminator 2*, a man selling chicken parts, Taco Bells, Reeboks again, Honda again, and several thousand other prod-ucts. It was free television and that meant the only people being paid had been paid in front.

The games continued on a dozen regional networks. Duke was a triumph over North Carolina State and out west, UCLA edged USC in a game of exquisite skill and daring in which young college men began to think like the pros.

The pros were ready as well with the Chicago Bulls pounding out a steamroller victory over the bad, bad Detroit Pistons and the New York Knicks slipping and sliding down the court until the Boston Celtics could make another notch on its collective gun belt with a fourteen-point blowout that blasted the spread to hell.

The games came in, rolling in all evening long, flashing up on the wall of television monitors in the various dim-lit chapels to the god of gambling in Las Vegas. The games consisted of sweat, blood, tears, heart, guts, soul, desire, motivation, and a dozen other words that inspire sportsmen to play and poets to write odes to the glory of it all. The games consisted of wagers in dark corners of dark saloons across the darkened countryside, of oddsmakers poring over their computers, laying off, balancing the action, beating the spread, making action that had a remote connection to the action on the courts.

And who controlled this juggernaut of games? No one. It was rolling down the hillside without brakes and without a driver.

Zebras in their striped shirts or gray pullovers were running up and down the hardwood courts in the pro leagues and college leagues and high school leagues, and they were watching for elbows, double dribbling, knees inside, and deliberate head checks and personal fouls of a ranker nature. The games consisted of thousands of players making hundreds of thousands of moves, and through it all, the zebras were watching to keep the games on the square, on the level, on the up-and-up.

They were as underpaid in this effort as good schoolteachers, mamas who do laundry for three dollars an hour, and poets who never sell their songs for as much as they are worth.

It was just another night, Wednesday or Thursday, and there was snow falling in parts of the country and rain falling in other parts and it was full of games.

THIRTY-THREE

L EO MYERS heard the noise before he saw anything. In fact, he didn't want to see anything.

He said, "Who is it?"

The answer was a thump, exactly like the thump of a silencer. Leo had heard that thump in a spy movie he watched one afternoon in Glasses saloon, some movie about a spy in New Orleans who killed the wrong guy or something. You know, thump and then another thump.

Leo's eyes were wide open in the darkness of his sleeping room but he couldn't see a thing. Because it was dark. Because he was dead.

Tommy Gallagher went down the back stairs of the four-flat, his tasseled loafers slipping on the snow, so he had to grip the wooden rail. Three flights down. The alley was full of life, rats and other animals pulling garbage duty. Two of the homeless winos were huddled in the shadow of a commerical dumpster, their worldly goods in two stolen supermarket shopping carts. One of them was awake, staring at Gallagher with drunken red eyes that were as mean as a rat's.

Gallagher almost slipped again and steadied himself with one gloved hand against the rough back brick of the hotel. The St. Philbert Arms was halfway between being a flop and a residential hotel of the better class. Just a place for someone like Leo.

There was snow on the BMW at the curb. Gallagher wiped at the back window with his gloved hand. The flakes were big, just barely on the cold side of being water.

He didn't see the man in the doorway across the street until the man stepped onto the walk. The side street was narrow with a line of cars parked on both sides. The opening down the middle of the street was just wide enough for one car.

"Hello, Tommy," the big man said.

Gallagher stared at him a moment and then grinned. "What the hell are you doing here, Captain?"

"Ah, I was after asking the same to you, Tommy," the captain said.

"Had to see someone," he said. He was waiting, still grinning, but waiting with the loose-limbed stance of a linebacker a moment before the snap.

"Who would that be?"

"Someone owed me some money. A little side money."

"I didn't know you drove one of these kraut cars."

"I picked it up in a drug auction a few months ago. Belonged to a Latin coke king. Rodriguez or something. He kept it nice. Didn't get to drive it much. And won't now for the next fifteen years in Marion."

"Ah." Nothing. "I was taking the night air. I don't sleep much at nights and there wasn't much on TV. Watched the DePaul game. DePaul beat up on the Irish."

"I saw some of it."

"I know. In that tavern. Glasses."

"You know Glasses." Waited. Let it go down between them. "You know I was there? Whyn't you come in for a drink?"

"Ah, I didn't want you to know I was there."

216

"You want to stand on the street talking, you want to go some place?"

"Street's fine. Not a soul out tonight in a storm unless they had a bad reason to be someplace," Carmody said. His voice was not growling. It was soft and menacing, exactly the voice he unconsciously found for himself when it was him and the bad guys in the old days. "I was talking tonight with Jimmy Drover."

"Is that right?"

"And a suit named Peterson. Federal Bureau of Investigation."

"Is that right?"

"Come off it, Tommy." Soft, as soft as snow burying a farmhouse in Kansas. Soft, soft, flake by flake, drop by drop, blotting out the world.

"Off what?"

"Who lives in that fleabag? Is it Leo Myers, Tommy?"

"Look, Captain. Leo Myers is a bad guy. He was fixing games, he was in the Outfit. You told Drover the Outfit was after his ass? I was trying to do him a favor."

"A favor."

"Favor for you, Cap. You called me into this."

"I did. That weighs on me, Tommy. I was the one called you in. And you was the one told someone about this girl, this Fionna girl, who got beat up night before, got beat up by Steve March."

"Who told you that?"

"Drover."

"Drover is smoking funny cigarettes or something."

"Tommy, what did you have to say to Leo just now? You was talking to him weren't you? Like you were old friends. Maybe very old friends."

"Captain. I knew Leo Myers, I busted him once. I—"

"You knew Dan Briggs too?"

"I didn't know no Dan Briggs."

"I was talkin' to this homicide dick, Cummings, wrote up the report on Dan Briggs. Suicide it was. Left a typewritten suicide note exactly matched the typewriter in his house. Why would someone type up a note instead of writing it out in his own hand?"

"Maybe he could type better than he could write. I dunno."

"Ah, Tommy, Tommy. What'd you get involved in?"

Gallagher said nothing.

The big man took a step.

"Tommy, the vowels. You got in with the vowels. What were you doing, fixing games? Was Briggs part of it?"

"When Marilou divorced me, she took me. Took the kids and took me. You know what my nut is?"

"You never see the kids."

"I got no time. I put that part of my life behind me."

"You're a cold bastard, Tommy, never see your own flesh."

"I put it behind me."

"Tommy, you're gonna do the right thing. You aren't going to be in this no more, are you?"

"Captain, this G., Peterson. He's putting a squeeze down. Tonight. He said he wants me to report to the federal building in the morning. Eight o'clock. Sent the word through the superintendent's office like I was a piece of shit. He wants to hang something on me. I don't have anything to do with Steve March, I swear I don't. I didn't tell him anything."

"Someone did, Tommy. You told someone."

"I was pushing Leo around, putting the fear on him."

"Why?"

"You sent Drover to me. He said Briggs was murdered. I wanted to see—"

"You're as full of shit as a Christmas goose, Tommy. You took out this Briggs fella, didn't you?"

Standing there, in the snowy street, two men talking to each other. A cab came sliding along, all dents and neglect. They stepped back while it passed.

"Briggs. Briggs was fixing games, Cap. Long before I got on the scene. He was working it with Leo Myers and Leo was letting his tax man in on it. Guy named Bugs Rio. Bugs was working for Steve March. So every now and then Briggs would shave a game to make it a dead-certain thing to beat the odds. He had his problems. Wife dead, lived alone, bought himself company. Whores. He was going downhill faster than I thought. Made three or four trips to Vegas every year. You know what I mean. Drinking, gambling, I pulled him up and told him to shape up. So you might say, I discovered what he was doing and I thought, why not get in on the action? So Steve didn't know about me, Leo didn't know about me at first. That made it too complicated. I needed him to book my action because if I started using another book, they'd get wise. I mean, if Steve March is collecting taxes from everyone."

"Sure, Tommy. That makes it more like it," Carmody said. His voice almost sounded relieved. "You were just shaking down a fix that was going on anyway, whether or not you were in on it."

"That's it, Captain," Gallagher said. He tried the grin again. And it was met by a grin. Two cops who understood each other. "The thing was that the more I got into it, the more I found out what it was. Briggs was working with a partner. Another zebra. They matched up together fairly often but they didn't want to fix too many games, just enough. A little here and there."

"Who was the other guy?"

"I don't want to say."

"Not to me. Not to Peterson."

"Exactly. Fucking Peterson screwed everything up, I didn't even know he existed. Then he calls me off when I was doing a pretend investigation of Drover's charges. You know how it goes. Stupid Leo must have panicked and told Bugs Rio who must have told Steve March. March did the wrong thing."

"He did. He did the wrong thing when he beat up Fionna Givens and when he beat up the woman cop a couple of years ago."

"Too bad it isn't the old days, Cap. We'd just go out and waste him, the way you used to do it," Gallagher said.

Carmody said nothing.

"Thing is, Peterson is building a case against Steve March and I don't even figure into this—"

"Except if Dan Briggs were alive to tell—"

"Naw. Briggs made a problem for himself. He got visited by this Peterson and that made him panic. And then he got called in by the NCAA and that really sent him off. He was telling Leo that he couldn't do this anymore, he was going to have to go clean, tell every-thing . . . See, Cap?"

"Confession. They always want to go clean at the worst times. Had someone like that once in the murder squad."

"Who?"

"It doesn't matter. We took care of our own problem."

The grin was wider now. "I like that, Captain. I did the same thing."

"You killed Dan Briggs and wrote up his suicide note."

"Had to be done."

"And who did you put the fear in? The other ref?"

"I didn't talk to the guy ever. I used Leo to tell the guy that Steve March didn't want no change because Dan Briggs had killed himself and that the fixes would go on. I mean, Briggs was making five grand a game."

"Who do you think put through the tip to the NCAA? You think it was Peterson?"

"Sure. Peterson puts on the squeeze and then he drops a note to the Double A and they add to the squeeze. I'd do the same thing same way if I was them," Gallagher said.

"So what are you gonna do now?"

"I'm going to have a drink at the Zebra. You feel like going out to have a drink?"

"My car is around the corner," Carmody said.

"Well, let me drive you. Close up the Zebra Lounge, I'll drive you to your car, we don't need two cars down there."

"But that takes you out of your way, Tommy. You live down around there. In a condo."

"Condo," Gallagher said. "I rent it."

"Ah yeah. That's right. Anyways, it takes you out of your way."

"I don't mind, Captain. I'm a little wired tonight. Still gotta face the G in the morning."

"Aren't you worried about this fella? I mean, the bookie? Only link to you is Leo Myers."

"Not anymore," Tommy Gallagher said.

Carmody stared at him and then nodded. "Just so," Carmody

said. "Well, I think you handled it well, Tommy. I just hate to see you doing business with the vowels."

"It was an opportunity. Besides, Cap, I didn't do business with them. Steve and Bugs never knew about the deal I was cutting myself in on. It was Briggs and Leo Myers and that was that."

"No Briggs now. And no Leo now, is that it?"

"That's it." Waiting again, agile and loose-limbed, waiting for the snap of the ball and the rush into the pit at the middle of the line.

But it didn't come. Carmody took a step and put his hand on Tommy's shoulder. The old man was nearly as big as the man with the linebacker's stance but the gesture made him larger. Tommy might be a kid who had a bad day in school for all the gesture meant.

"Lad, I think you ought to see your kids. Take them out for a weekend. Take them up to Great America or someplace. Be a father to them."

"I'll do it, Cap."

"Tommy. Tommy, you didn't tell the vowels about Fionna? Drover said you tol' the vowels."

"Bring her in? Why would I do that? It must of been Leo Myers, lookin' around for something to see what made Drover tick. I wouldn't put a woman in harm's way, Cap, you know that."

"I know that. I was just asking."

"And I'm just telling. Jeez. That makes me sick, you think that about me."

"I don't think it about you, Tommy. But let this be a lesson. Don't get involved with them. Not even close to them. They don't trust each other, they got no souls, they got no respect for women. They wouldn't trust each other, let alone someone from outside. You understand me, Tommy?"

Tommy nodded.

A long silence.

"Good lad then."

The hand was removed from his shoulder.

"We'll take your car then. We'll have a couple of jars then. I don't think I been in the Zebra Lounge since I was retired."

"Treat's on me, Cap," Gallagher said, smiling in a curious way, wondering if that was all there was to it.

"On you then," Carmody said. "I never could of been a lawyer, you know, because I couldn't pass a bar."

They were smiling, chuckling, old friends, student and mentor and all the rest of it. The BMW was smooth and the engine growled just enough to make pedestrians notice. It was an animal, prowling through empty streets streaked with fallen snow. Just like an animal. It was going to be all right.

THIRTY-FOUR

HE KNOCKED at her door again shortly after dawn. The sky was red and clear. The cornfields were as beautiful as a new-made world under the burden of white snow. The snow had purified everything and it excited them, even the crusty old farmers who gathered for coffee in the country stores, thrilled them exactly as snow thrills the child in almost everyone. City snow is an obstruction but country snow is peace on earth, goodwill to men.

Fionna was dressed, waiting for him. They had talked before but they were not talked out. Not yet.

"I called Neil after Paul was out of danger and he was shocked. I knew he was shocked. He said no one kills himself over a game. It's only a game, he said. It was the same kind of thing you said to me. Remember? In the coffeehouse where you took me? You said Dan Briggs didn't kill himself because of an anonymous charge against him."

"He didn't. He was killed."

"You said that but you don't know who did it."

"No. But what about Paul?"

She told him. She had promised Paul not to tell anyone and she told Drover because Paul had tried to kill himself. Promises were off.

"What's wrong with him?" Drover said.

It wasn't what she expected.

Drover got up and went to the window. She was sitting on her unmade bed and she stared at his back. He looked through the blinds at the whiteness of the countryside. "It's pretty," he said to himself. "I forgot how pretty it was after it snowed. Walking across the quad to classes, throwing snowballs like we were seven years old."

"Why did you say that?"

"It's a fucking game, Fionna. It isn't life. He didn't do anything wrong. Neil did the violation and they can't touch Neil now, he's on television. The golden afterlife. So one little violation isn't going to pull down the empire of St. Mary's."

"He took it on himself. He blamed himself for turning a blind eye. He said he should have known something—"

Drover turned to her. "He tried to kill himself. Maybe. He took Valium but he made sure you knew he was on the verge of doing something crazy. You called the North Fork fire department and it was no contest, Paul was not going to die. But he sure drew attention to himself. The holy martyr. One day little Dorothy goes behind the curtain and finds out the Wizard of Oz is a carny faker."

"He said they all had to know—Father O, Dave Zekman, he just couldn't live with that burden of—"

"Give me a break, Fionna."

She was setting her pretty jaw against him. She had wept in his arms at midnight and now it was morning and midnight never happened.

"Paul is a baby and you were babying him. All the time. You were Mother and he was in diapers. He married another baby. They lived forever and ever happily in the enchanted campus of St. Mary's College. This is not a fairy tale, Fionna. I take the blame. You got beaten by some crazy man because I trusted a kinky cop. I am sorry. I am heartily sorry as we said in the Act of Contrition. I am sorry for Dan Briggs who was shot to death with his own gun. I am sorry for

Albert Brown who took the money. He might be some jock from Nowhere, North Carolina, but he knows the value of money. He saw his mama make it three dollars at a time and when the white dude dropped hundreds and thousands of the stuff on them, Albert was smart enough to keep his mouth shut."

"You slept with me. I feel dirty about it."

Drover stared at her. "Why, Fionna? You used me as a Judas goat, why feel dirty now? You dumped Paul's problem on me, you dumped your husband's philandering on me, you came to my room one night. Why wouldn't I make love to you? I had a crush on you going back fifteen years. And you're beautiful, Fionna, as pretty as your name. You really are breaking hearts every day, you know. Take mine, for instance."

"Is that supposed to make up for what you've said?"

He shook his head. "I hate the truth nearly as much as you do. I just have to deal with it more often."

"Gamblers and bookies and oddsmakers. That's the truth, huh?"

"Getting TV contracts, buying meat for the team at so much per pound, telling pure, untutored athletes that this is their ticket to the NBA . . . Christ, Fionna, what do you think college sports is all about? There's a fairy tale you and Paul and Betsy and Father O crawl inside to make nice to yourselves."

She was so mad she could cry. So she did. Burning hot tears, just like anger. She got up and hit him hard across the face.

Winced. The pain from her taped ribs turned her face white and she stumbled against him. He caught her and held her.

"It hurt," she said.

"Take it easy, Fionna." He just stood and held her and she let him hold her.

"Paul's ruined his life," she said.

"He wants someone to tell him it isn't ruined."

"But no one will."

Drover held her and thought about it the way he had thought about it all night.

"Let me take you to the hospital."

"I don't need a hospital."

"To see Paul."

"I don't know what to tell him."

"Maybe you can think of something," Drover said.

She pushed away from him and he let her go. "You're mean, Jimmy, just mean. I didn't think you were mean once. You've just gotten mean with what you do."

"No. I don't think so," Drover said. "Maybe it was the crush. I told you about it. The one that worked on me again as though all these years hadn't gone by. You were just there, very pretty and sure. I used to watch your mouth, you had the prettiest, most interesting mouth."

"Don't do that," she said.

"All right. You go on your own to the hospital. I've got a thing or two to do."

"You've done enough things."

Drover said nothing. He went to the door and let himself out. Morning light filled the corridor from windows at the east end. He felt sadness tugging like a street urchin at his elbow.

THIRTY-FIVE

C ARY LUCAS was travel-worn, the way someone gets at the end of a week on the road when there are more dirty clothes in your bag than clean and home is still a thousand miles and a few stops away. It showed in those Minnesota blue eyes and the lines at the corners of his mouth.

"How'd you know where to find me?" he said to Drover. They were standing at the door that separates the terminal building from the apron. The twin-engine jet was huffing and puffing on the tarmac, waiting for the next leg of the journey to begin. Six more takeoffs and landings before the middle of the afternoon and a fuel break at O'Hare. The twenty-five-minute commute to North Fork had been as smooth as going up an escalator and then going down.

"Called NBA headquarters in Washington. I was Dave Zekman this time and wanted to know who was coming down to investigate Paul Givens."

"They told you me."

"You were the logical man."

"I was going home today. Why the hell would a guy resign as coach and then go and kill himself?"

"Look, Cary. I want to be straight with you."

"Yeah sure. I circulated your real name around back in D.C. and they said you were some kind of troubleshooter for a Vegas odds-maker named Fox Vernon. I shouldn't even talk to you. We shouldn't breathe the same air."

"I know you're better than me. I've been meeting a lot of people like that. I wonder if it means I'm going downhill or they think they're on the wrong floor," Drover said.

"Smart guy."

"Exactly. I've got some stuff for you that you won't get for a while. You look tired. Let's sit down and drink a cup of airport coffee and see if we've got anything to trade."

Cary Lucas made a sour look using his eyes, nose, and mouth, but he followed Drover to the coffee shop at one end of the terminal. A waitress named Dixie—it said it on her name tag—brought mugs of java and nondairy creamer. Cary and Drover decided to keep the coffee black.

"What do we have to talk about?"

"I want to know who tipped you about trouble with the St. Mary's team. I mean, all the stuff, the bullshit about players shaving games, the stuff about Albert Brown. The recruiting violation stuff."

"That's impossible."

"Look, I know you know. And I guess."

"Go ahead and guess."

"How about Dave Zekman?"

"How about him."

"Why would he do it?"

"I don't know that he did it."

"I called Fox Vernon yesterday and he went back over some stuff. Nexis. It's a computer library you can tap into, get stuff from a lot of newspapers. I wanted him to look into Santa Fe University over the past, say, four years, after Dave Zekman left there for his job at St. Mary's."

"Yes?"

"There's a very serious investigation that isn't going anywhere. Involving payoffs to players at Santa Fe, outright gifts of cars, jobs, spending money, the usual shit. Foxy checked around in Las Vegas among the kind of people who gamble for a living."

"Some living."

"This was going back to Dave Zekman's day. When Dave was A.D. it was more than four years ago."

"Was it?"

"Damnit, Cary, listen to me. I want to get a guy out of the trouble he made for himself and the only way I can do it is help you. For helping me."

"I can't give away a confidence. How can you help me?"

"NCAA dropped the Santa Fe investigation more or less, didn't they?"

"All right."

"Because Dave Zekman gave you something better."

"Is that right?"

"Tell me if that's right."

"I can't tell you anything."

"Look, why did the Double A go public with the news about the St. Mary's investigation? What changed?"

"Nothing. We wanted to narrow the field down. Lot of wild charges going around. The tip on point shaving was bullshit."

"Cary, Paul Givens's world was blown away last night when he tried to kill himself."

Cary stared. It was a cop stare and there wasn't any mercy in it.

"Give him his life back."

"How do I do that?"

"I'll tell you." And that's what Drover did. He betrayed Paul's secret conversation with Albert Brown, right down to going to Dave Zekman and Zekman telling him he didn't want to know anything.

Cary Lucas studied his hands wrapped around the mug of mud. He looked out the window at the snowscape. "Going to be a long winter starting this early," he said. He said it like a farmer. There was a wistful note in his voice. He kept looking out the window, not at Drover.

"I don't know who sent in all the original stuff but I could figure it out after a while. Dave said he wanted to cooperate, that Paul and Neil were as thick as thieves in recruiting when he came there and that if we could see our way clear to save his ass—save his reputation at Santa Fe—he would cooperate with us at St. Mary's. Tit for tat. The decision wasn't made by me. There're all kinds of factors weighed in something like this. So Dave cooperated good. He showed me that Neil O'Neill was drawing down slush money. A lot of slush right out of the athletic department. And it was coming out of Paul Givens's account too and he thought it was going for recruiting or for Neil's life-style."

"Dave could have gone to the police if he thought Neil was stealing money."

"Sure. So he didn't. That means he thought it was being used for other things. He said he had been so tied up with changing around the football program his first two years as athletic director he didn't have time to monitor the accounts of the basketball side."

"Good, I like that. Saint Dave turning state's evidence," Drover said.

"Dave Zekman is neither the best nor the worst. Man, you should know what I know about some of these big-money programs. Get a state university with real power, real connections going out to everyone from company chairmen to auto dealers who want to spread their gifts around. This thing is so crooked, Drover, it couldn't be straightened out with a forge."

Drover joined him in staring at the fields of snow. It was sparkling in the clear, cold sunlight. "I know," Drover said. "Neil gave Albert Brown money. Or his mother."

"I know," Cary said. "Mama told me. Couple of hundred bucks. I thought about what you said. Yeah, hell. No use ruining a man's life over a couple of hundred bucks. Besides, a mistake like that . . . well, no one wants St. Mary's ass that bad."

Drover thought about it. Shook his head. "Just a couple of hundred bucks. Zekman sure had it in for Paul Givens."

"He's an average shark. Not a great white and not a porpoise. Just a shark chewing up what comes in his way. College campuses breed it. Like incest. They're always plotting and counterplotting, it's kind of silly."

"Paul tried to kill himself because he had a breakdown. Paranoia as a fact of faculty life. He thought everyone was against him. He talked to Albert Brown and Albert told him that he had received some money, his mother had or someone had—"

"His mother. Nice lady. Hard, hard life. Ought to see where they live. They burn logs in the winter," Cary said. Shook his head.

"You can't touch Neil. Don't have to hurt Paul."

"Maybe not."

"I take that as a yes."

"You don't know. I might change my mind."

"I don't think so. Thing is, there's Dave Zekman."

"I won't do his dirty for him. He wants to get rid of Paul, he **can** do it like a man and not use NCAA."

"That's the point, Cary. He was using you from jump street. Just one other thing. What about the zebra. Who turned in the zebra to you?"

"Dan Briggs?"

Drover looked at him.

Cary looked at the dregs of his coffee and shook his head as Dixie approached with a pot of regular and a pot of decaf. Drover did the same.

"Briggs. Himself. He said he was shaving and he wanted to turn himself in.

"Briggs himself."

"It was serious and we were trying to figure out how to handle it when we got interfered with by the FBI which told us to down-hold any investigation involving Dan Briggs. They had something going on that was priority. So we waited a couple of weeks and Briggs got nervous and asked me to see him. I saw him. I couldn't tell him anything and it made me mad but it made him very, very jumpy. I didn't understand it. Then he died."

"Got killed."

"I don't know that," Cary Lucas said.

"Okay. You were as straight with me as you could be."

"What are you going to do?"

"Talk to my father confessor," Drover said.

"About what?"

"The quality of forgiveness. It's the thing that makes us humans instead of animals," Drover said, rising.

"Yeah. I might have read that in a book, it sounds so phony," Cary Lucas said.

THIRTY-SIX

T HEY LAID it out for Lt. Thomas Gallagher in the morning.

They started with coffee and rolls on a bare table in a bare room on the nineteenth floor of the Everett M. Dirksen federal building in the Loop.

They tried to booga-booga but Tommy Gallagher once led a platoon of Marines into a village of booby traps and Cong and personally Zippoed the first thatched roof and personally shot down every boy in black pajamas and didn't let it interfere with his sleep. He was that tough.

When they couldn't do it that way, they tried Federal Agent Looks One Through Six on him and he let it roll off him. He drank coffee until it was gone and then didn't ask for more. Never ask, never explain.

They didn't have shit except for a dead bookie in a flophouse and that wasn't anything at all.

THIRTY-SEVEN

FOURTEEN ARRESTS were made that morning and afternoon. They took Steve March out of his brick bungalow in Elmwood Park after the kids went to school but while his wife was still there. She cried, screamed, and spit at them and Steve March just smiled.

Bugs Rio was already laying out the rest of it. He was glad it was over. Ten months on a wire, ten months of watching his back with a psychopath like Steve March. He told them everything he could, right down to Steve March beating up Fionna Givens because she had hired a Vegas guy to look into the death of a referee. Scare them off because it might interfere with a nice racket. Two refs, Dan Briggs and a guy named Sonterro who were doing quiet little fixes against the point spread. Blow a whistle here, catch a traveling call there when traveling was the only way to go. Just keep it simple, don't upset the games or upset the Vegas bookmakers with bets that were too big. Keep it simple and let the money roll in, maybe eighty thousand a season if they were lucky. Half to Steve March, 10 percent each to the refs, nothing to Leo Myers who had to book the bets for his usual 10 percent vig.

Peterson thought it would be funny for Steve March to see Bugs Rio, see what their reactions would be. It was hilarious. Steve was in manacles but he went for Bugs anyway, his eyes practically came out of his sockets, the G-men thought it was worth it. Funny. They talked about it for weeks after, about the way Steve practically hit Bugs and Bugs looked like he was going to have a heart attack. Steve made bail by putting up a quarter million cash and Bugs began to learn the intricacies of the U.S. Witness Protection Program. For the time of his life left after he testified. Against Steve, against a whole range of bookmakers, gamblers, juice men, the whole network. It was called Operation Gambscan because these things always have to have a name to be used by the media.

THIRTY-EIGHT

FATHER O'BRIEN was drinking a little whiskey in a little water. Just a little to settle his nerves. His face was as white as his hair on this long, excruciating winter afternoon.

Drover sat in the leather chair by the fireplace and talked it all out, right down to Father O'Brien and Dave Zekman letting Paul Givens dangle in the wind. No one wanted bad publicity for St. Mary's athletic program. But no one wanted to know anything either.

"I can't," the priest said finally. "You were here, Mr. Drover. You must have some loyalty to the school."

"I'm not a very loyal guy," Drover said.

"You did what you did for Fionna."

"She asked me. She wanted to save her brother from a setup. What do you want out of your program? You hire a shark like Dave Zekman and you let him feed on Paul."

"I had the decision to appoint Paul as basketball coach. I did that."

"Because Neil put a choke hold on you. I hate to say this, but the only guy who seemed to know the right thing to do all along was Neil."

"Neil is not a very honorable person the way you make him out," Father O'Brien said.

"Why? Because he knew you were giving him the old wink and nod to go out and recruit some bodies for the team with whatever methods he could rustle up? Neil didn't feel bad about it but he had some decent instincts. He gave Fionna the house as a going-away present when he left her. He gave the job to Paul for the same reason. I'm guessing this but I like to think I'm right."

"Well, he didn't help Paul out when he lied to the NCAA. When he said Paul had recruited Albert Brown and worked out the arrangements. That was a lie."

"It was a bald-faced lie. It was a lie big enough to be shot down by anyone who looked at it twice. Cary Lucas went to North Carolina and the lie dissolved like tissue paper. So Neil let himself be tarred as the bad guy and he didn't care. He expected you'd stand by Paul. The world is just full of stand-up guys like you, Father. You walk away from it as soon as you see the guy is ready to take the bullet himself. Paul was left standing alone and you didn't lift a finger for him."

"He did what he thought was best—"

"He was torn up. He knew he never did a bad thing. That's a terrible burden for an adult, to know you really still believe in goodness."

Father O'Brien said nothing. The whiskey tasted too much like water. The beautiful afternoon was tinged with melancholy in the red rim of the horizon where the sun was setting. Too early. The days were short. Melancholy embraced the old priest's shoulders.

"Give him the job," Drover said.

"I won't kick him out. He's part of the faculty—"

"Let him coach Neil's team. After all, he was the only one who didn't pay for it unless he had died last night."

"I never knew those things."

"Father, it's been a long time since I believed in keeping your innocence by sticking your head in the sand. You knew what you were doing the minute you hired on Dave Zekman to work the program.

238

'Maximize revenues.' Show the board of governors a nice balance sheet and a hefty profit. Football team goes to the Orange Bowl and St. Mary's is on the road to the Final Four in March. Let him be part of it and when St. Mary's gets slapped—if it does get slapped—take it like a man. Yourself."

"I didn't do anything."

"You hired Dave Zekman and turned your back on Paul," Drover said. "You did the wrong thing."

"Dave Zekman is not a bad man."

"No one's bad but one man is good. Goodness is its own reward but it doesn't have to be punished too." He wouldn't take the blame.

The priest went to the window. His bones were cold. The fiery sunset was casting long shadows across the quad. The chapel bells rang. Students followed footpaths in the snow across the quad, from building to building. Always the same, always hopeful, always preparing for a tomorrow.

"I'll think about it."

"Think about it. Pray on it. Do the right thing."

"If I keep Paul, I lose Dave Zekman."

"He wasn't your friend. He wasn't a friend to St. Mary's. He tainted the program to get rid of it. He plied rumors. He was behind those anonymous charges about St. Mary's basketball players' shaving games. It wasn't true and the only harm it did was to burden Paul Givens to the point where he couldn't take it anymore," Drover said.

"You were . . . a good friend of his." The priest turned. "You're very loyal to your friends."

Drover let it go. If the priest wanted to think he was Paul's friend, it might make it easier.

"You're right, I suppose," Father O'Brien said. "Right. And when I tell Dave Zekman, what have I lost?"

"No."

The priest stared at him.

"What did you find?" Drover said. "Maybe the right thing you almost lost."

THIRTY-NINE

V<small>IN BROUGHT</small> a big plate of spaghetti over to the kitchen table in the immense white kitchen and set it down. Tony Rolls had a restaurant kitchen in his house because he liked restaurant food and didn't like people he didn't know staring at him when he ate.

"Good, good," he said to Vin, gesturing with his fork. "Siddown, Vin, pour the wine, let's eat and enjoy our lives."

"You heard about the cop?"

"I didn't hear nothing. I was listening to Sinatra in the study, I must of fallen asleep. What news is that you're speakin' of?"

Vin looked at the old man in the wheelchair and then pulled up a seat in front of his own plate. He ate with a fork in one hand, a knife in the other and a torn piece of good Italian bread on the side of his plate.

"Cop was whacked in Carmenino's coffee shop on Aberdeen Street this afternoon. Guy walked in and blew his face off."

"What cop was this?"

"Cop named Gallagher. Tommy Gallagher."

Tony Rolls chewed it over with his spaghetti. He had large yellow teeth and a big jaw that got bigger as the rest of his face shrunk with age. "No kiddin'."

"Everyone is announcing this investigation and that. Nobody seen nothin'."

"Of course."

"Gallagher was the cop was called in when Leo Myers the book was found shot. Someone says they say this Gallagher was going to turn evidence, so they whacked him."

"I don' follow all this stuff no more. Nobody tells me nothin'. They treat me with respect but not with real respect, you know? Like they don' wanna tell me nothing'."

"You're still a big man, Tony. The biggest."

"Eh." He rolled his head, shaking off the compliment but doing it carefully so that the gleam of it stuck. He liked compliments. Everyone did. It was natural.

"Who you think whacked him?" Vin said.

"I wouldn't know. It was crazy, whacking a cop. That's the work of someone who isn't thinking square. I never heard that Gallagher was a guy who was workin' with us. I never heard that but then, no one tells me nothin. You ever hear that, Vin, when you're out partying?"

"I know that Gallagher put some heat on that bookie that died. And the G called him in a couple of times after they put down Steve March."

"Steve March wasn't careful. He trusted Bugs Rio, that wasn't careful. He scared Bugs all the time, I know that. You got to proceed on trust, Vin, you got to put your faith in people who will do you the right way because you do them the right way. Capeesh?"

"Yeah," Vin said. He tore another piece of bread from the loaf between them. He spooned giardiniera on his plate and dipped the bread in the oil and hot peppers.

"Steve March has got a wife and two children, he should of been careful about things but he was too hot in the head all the time. It was a matter of time, someone would have whacked Steve or something like what happened with the G would happen. The G ain't stupid."

"They ain't stupid," Vin said. He thought they were. But the old man wasn't really conversing anyway, just thinking out loud.

"Matter of time. I wonder who whacked this Gallagher?" Rhetorical.

They both thought they knew.

FORTY

BLACK KELLY made the salmon fillet in the dishwasher and it was very, very good.

He served Nancy Harrington first and then Lori Gibbons and then Drover and then Neil O'Neill. Because Neil agreed to fly down from San Francisco where he was doing the color on the 49ers game the day after Christmas, they had made Christmas Eve serve as Christmas Day.

It suited Lori too. She had called four days earlier, out of the blue, and announced she was off the New York–Tokyo run because she had seen enough and because she might be getting ready to settle down. Into being a microbe hunter or something. She had clear eyes, a clear voice, a great figure, fine skin, and was perfect except for the slight overbite that called attention to all her other attributes. She was the late actress Lee Remick as a young woman, classy and sexy without even trying. She had once been a quarterback's girlfriend and then she and Drover had had a thing or two. They were friends, as they say. Maybe more, maybe not as much as people would think.

Neil O'Neill turned compliments like a blackjack dealer turning cards. Drover was fascinated and he smiled as Nancy and Lori in turn took his honey words and smoothed them over themselves.

"Neil, you're a dangerous man to invite. Nancy and Kelly are friends and Lori called me to see me at Christmas, not you," Drover said.

Neil smiled like a million dollars. "See, Lori, he's jealous if anyone says what's just the truth. He's feeling inadequate, forlorn, he wishes he had worked on his Charles Atlas exercises more when he was young instead of reading books."

"He reads a lot of books," Lori said. "So do I."

"I don't," Neil said. "I'm a dumb ex-jock. I just know what pleases the eye and both of you are candles on a banquet table."

"Like the girls who posed as mermaids that time at the Super Bowl. The big hotel guy, ah, Hilton was throwing a private bash like he does for five thousand close friends," Black Kelly said. "Had a long table with seafood on it, crabs, lobster, you know, and at either end, as table decorations, two half-naked girls posing as mermaids."

"I remember that," Neil said. "I stole a grand from the athletic budget and treated Fionna and me in New Orleans that weekend."

"That sounds chauvinist," Lori said. She would say things like that, out of the blue.

"What? Treating my then-wife to a weekend?"

"No. Using live models as table decorations."

Drover said, "It is chauvinist. That's what sports are all about."

"Sports is about money," Neil said.

"I'll drink to that," Drover said. They clinked glasses around the table. The bar was shut for the evening. Even non-Christians were told to go home and prepare for the coming of the Christ Child.

Lori said, "I've been looking at money. A girl thinks about that. But money comes with strings on it. I was pitched all the way to Japan and all the way back by some gorgeous hunks with money around them."

"And?"

Lori smiled, let the overbite flash. "Money isn't everything, is it, Nancy?"

"Not when you can have a man cook your Christmas dinner in a dishwasher," Nancy Harrington said. She had had hard times and the good times she had now were owed to her. She worked for Kelly but they were more like partners, the way they treated each other. They were both still in the awkward stage of whatever they were becoming, still cautious but filled with mutual admiration.

"I never thought I'd see you again," Drover said to Lori Gibbons.

"I never expected to see you. I guess it was getting close to Christmas and I was thinking of someone I wanted to spend the day with, someone who was a pretty good person." She also said things like "pretty good person." She got away with it on sincerity points. "I guess the good ones are already taken. You ever think that, Nancy?"

"I know it," Nancy said. "Present company excepted."

"It was nice of you to invite me down," Neil said to Drover. "Both of you."

"We wanted a TV star as a centerpiece when we found out the mermaids had been done," Drover said. "You were not invited because you were a good person, Neil."

"Naw, I know that. I'm just average. Okay. Good persons we should know." He held up his glass. He stared right at Drover. "Good old Paul Givens getting his job back."

"Yeah," Drover said.

"Is that the basketball coach who tried to kill himself?" Lori Gibbons said. Nancy shuddered at that. Her Johno had killed himself and it had very nearly killed her. But that was part of the bad times and they were definitely behind her.

Kelly opened another bottle of Taittinger. The cork hit the ceiling.

"You're supposed to do that quietly, with élan," Drover said.

"Élan don't live here, Nancy does."

For some reason they thought carols would be nice. Not safe and snug inside the closed saloon on the pier but right out there on the boardwalk leading into the ocean under a clear California Christmas sky. It was cool but not cold and they shivered anyway. Kelly carried the bottle and the rest carried glasses full of champagne. They tried "Silent Night" and "God Rest Ye Merry Gentlemen"; and it turned out that Neil O'Neill had a very nice tenor voice and could carry a tune. Nancy, of course, had been a saloon singer in the bad old days in Vegas. Lori was flat but she kept it to herself.

God rest ye merry, indeed.

They stayed up through the magic night and talked and talked and talked and it felt good to talk things out, talk about anything. They remembered childhoods and chestnuts roasting and they even got tears in their eyes at different times.

And once, just once, Neil O'Neill cornered Drover.

"You did it for Fionna."

"All right," Drover said.

"It was all right what you did."

"It was all right, I guess. Messy."

"Everything is. You see, don't you? I mean, about me and Fionna."

"Yes."

"You really do, don't you?"

"Yes."

Neil stared at him, wavered a little, held on to the wall like a drunk.

"You really see," a drunk's repetition.

"It doesn't matter."

"I won't hit on Lori Gibbons."

"I'm not afraid of you." Drover smiled.

"Shit." Neil shook his head. He really was drunk. "You're bulletproof, right?"

"So far."

"Because your heart is pure."

"Not hardly, Neil."

"Ah come on. You like to be the good guy. It shows all over you, even when you don't think you're showing it."

"Chump. Like Paul."

"Naw. He keeps his heart pure by burying it."

"Come on, Neil, you're drunk. Let's go drink some more."

"Okay, Okay. I just wanted to tell you you weren't fooling any-one."

"Least of all you," Drover said.

"It takes one to know one."

And that was the truth at last.

POSTSCRIPT

ST. MARY'S Bulldogs lost to Duke in the semifinal game of the Final Four played at Indianapolis at the end of March.

They had a good run at it all through the play-offs. Each play-off game they advanced meant about a half million more in shared NCAA television dollars for the school.

Dave Zekman was picked up by one of the biggest state schools in the East right after the final of the Final Four games and he broke his contract with St. Mary's by mutual consent. Father George O'Brien praised him publicly for the fine job he had done with both major St. Mary's teams. (The football team had beaten Clemson in the Orange Bowl and finished number four in the national rankings.)

Paul Givens was scheduled to give a series of inspirational talks across the country in late spring and early summer about coping with "Christian despair." A book on the subject—tentatively entitled "When Jesus Isn't There"—was scheduled for spring publication the following year. It was being written by a sportswriter with the *Indi-*

anapolis News because Paul Givens couldn't write a letter without coaching.

Fionna Givens? She lives in an apartment—a different apartment—in Chicago and she began dating a lawyer with the public defender's office around the end of the basketball season. She introduced him to Paul and Paul made him feel welcome. Paul was making everyone feel welcome with his positive, God-always-loves-you-no-matter-what, approach to living. Betsy was expecting their third child. It all faintly nauseated Fionna but she kept smiling through. She finally started to dye her hair so that the grey didn't show anymore. She was, in every respect, beginning to act her age.

Drover and Kelly and Nancy are still hanging out in Kelly's red meat emporium on the big pier in Santa Cruz. Drover still works for Foxy from time to time. He wrote a letter to Carmody after Tommy Gallagher was whacked and Carmody never responded to it.

Other things happened.

Baseball season was limbering up in Florida and Arizona and everyone said the Cubs had a shot at it this year but Vegas put them 50–1 against winning the pennant. That was about right.

Oh.

Lori Gibbons got a crush on a merchant marine tofu-food nut in Baltimore and seriously thought about following him to the ends of his earth. But just in the nick of time, she was scheduled on the Chicago–San Francisco run and spent a few hilarious nights with Drover. What the hell. He wasn't much but he was fun.